# Praise for Greg Chapman

**For *The Last Night of October***

"*The Last Night of October* sees auth[illegible] g not only his best work to date but [illegible] st story of 2013."—*Scaryminds*

**For *Vaudeville***

"A fable for the modern age, Greg Chapman shows a strong grasp of the modern narrative."—*Scaryminds*

"*Vaudeville* is a great horror story that touches on themes of sorrow, alienation and loss." —*Horror Addicts*

"The greatest hook with *Vaudeville* is probably its cavalcade feel—that sense of carnival tied with innocence whose roots are to be found in tales like Bradbury's *Something Wicked This Way Comes*."—*Hellnotes*

**General**

"Greg Chapman is a new voice in horror and brings fresh angles to our genre, which too often recycles unoriginal stories. There is a cinematic quality to his storytelling, which lodges itself in your imagination, deepening the bold and disturbing tales he delivers."—Rocky Wood, Bram Stoker Award-winning author of *Stephen King: A Literary Companion*

"I've been an unabashed fan of Greg Chapman's extraordinary fiction since I read his first book, *The Noctuary*, and what I said about that book applies to all of his work—it's elegant, violent, witty, and packs an emotional wallop."—Lisa Morton, multi-Bram Stoker Award®-winner.

# GREG CHAPMAN'S BOOKS PUBLISHED BY IFWG

Midnight Masquerade (2023)
Black Days and Bloody Nights (2024)

# MIDNIGHT MASQUERADE

BY GREG CHAPMAN

Midnight Masquerade



ISBN-13: 978-1-922856-42-5



V1.0

Stories are original to this book, except: *The Last Night of October* (Bad Moon Books, 2013), *Left on October Lane* (Specul8 Publishing, 2018), Octoberville (*The End of Halloween*, 2016), and *Vaudeville* (Dark Prints Press, 2012).



Cover and internal art by Greg Chapman.

Printed in Palatino Linotype and Built Titling.

IFWG Publishing Australia
Gold Coast
www.ifwgaustralia.com

## Dedication

For Dad


## Acknowledgments

Many people helped me bring these particular nightmares to the page with their advice, guidance, and support. My wife Gwenda and my daughters, Abbi and Leah, who always understand my need to write. I also need to thank Lisa Morton for her humbling testimonial and Dan Russell and Tim Marquitz for their early advice on the new stories. Thanks as well to Lee Murray and Rebecca Rowland for their stellar testimonials. I also need to acknowledge the incredible IFWG crew, namely Publisher Gerry Huntman, and Noel Osualdini and Steve McCracken. Thank you so much for letting me share my dark and depraved imagination.

# TABLE OF CONTENTS

# INTRODUCTION

## BY LISA MORTON

I should probably start this with a full disclosure: I've done an introduction before for a Greg Chapman book (*The Last Night of October*, when it was released as a stand-alone novella by Bad Moon Books).

If you think this means I like Greg's work, you're dead on. I've liked it from the start, and it's been a distinct pleasure watching him grow and garner acclaim over the years that we've known each other.

What do I enjoy about his work? Well, first off, I think it's no coincidence that he's a gifted artist because his written work is also visual, painting with words instead of brushes or pixels. He often writes about colorful, even strangely gleeful locations, whether the ethereal stage of dead troubadours or the Halloween town of Octoberville.

But I think what I enjoy most about Greg's writing is that it all seems deeply rooted in morality and choice. Horror fiction is often described as the most transgressive of genres; apparently, we're not supposed to talk about subjects like death or bodily breakdown or fear, so those things have become the grist of horror and the subjects that make it the unruly child of the literary world. Many writers use this "get out of transgressive jail free" card to create horror fiction meant to gratuitously shock or disgust, and although there's certainly a place for "extreme" horror, it's not my thing.

It's not Greg Chapman's, either. His characters may experience these transgressive events, or even engage in them—see, for example, the terrible thing the protagonist of *The Last Night of October* did once, or the almost casual act of childhood cruelty that forms the background of "Thirty Years Later"—but that's not what his stories are about. Yes, the tried-and-true horror trope of a villain who receives a comeuppance figure into these stories, but Greg's work is too smart to simply end with a supernatural force delivering justice at the story's climax.

Instead, these tales often give the perpetrator of some past sin a chance at forgiveness. The person who once caused terrible harm is offered a shot at repentance…and the surprise—maybe even the ultimate transgression—is that they don't always accept, or even want, that offer. The aging clown who is finally pushed too far in the bleakly funny "Happy Daze" is given multiple chances to put his rage aside, but he doesn't…although perhaps his final act ultimately redeems a life of unhappy passivity. The woman who is buffeted between moral choices in the title story is told by the mysterious forces controlling her, "We gave you a choice: either salvation or damnation. It's how you chose." The stranded motorist of "Octoberville" triumphs over his nightmarish situation simply by accepting. In the final novella, "Vaudeville," a boy does take an offer of salvation, but soon discovers he's made a terrible mistake…or has he? Making the right decision isn't always as easy as it might at first seem.

Speaking of morality, Greg is plainly suspicious of organized religion, especially in "Second Chance Circus," when a priest finds he fits right in among torturers who refer to religion as "a shared madness", and "The History of Halloween," in which a Halloween expert (whose name happens to sound strangely like mine) is caught between her rigidly fundamentalist upbringing (which is something I thankfully do not share with this character) and the pagan roots of Halloween. In much horror fiction Christian values triumph over the forces of darkness, but Greg—like his spiritual father Clive Barker—finds that true morality is often ground under the heel of godly righteousness.

I had read a number of these stories before, and it was a pleasure to revisit those I was already acquainted with as well as partake of the new offerings in this collection. If this is your first time sampling Greg's work, welcome; if you, like me, are already a fan, you'll find *Midnight Masquerade* a fine reminder of why Greg is one of horror fiction's true dark delights.

Lisa Morton
Los Angeles,
December, 2022

Gerald saw one of the shadows beneath the tree move...

# THE LAST NIGHT OF OCTOBER

## 1

Every Halloween, Gerald Forsyth's worst fear would come a-knocking.

His existence was one of silent dread: a slow, steady tick of days until that last night of October. It was his every thought, every beat of his tired, old heart.

Gerald sat in his wheelchair, inside the living room of his modest home, slumped and breathless, oxygen mask clamped over his mouth, and stared at his front door. It would come soon: the very moment the sun disappeared beneath the horizon. It came without fail and, without fail Gerald would cower in the corner of his living room and pray for the sun to return.

He took several deep breaths, trying to subdue the anxiety swelling inside his chest. Ironically, the oxygen became too much for his wasted lungs and he was forced to pull the mask from his face. He began to cough, his old body bucking with each exertion. Gerald Forsyth was drowning on his own lungs. A moment later and the coughing fit passed. He sucked in more air and the action quickly equalized him—at least temporarily. He wiped the sweat from his leathery face and refocused on the front door.

*It will be here any minute,* he thought to himself. *You have to be ready. You've handled it many times before and you can do it again.* Gerald checked his watch—5:31pm. Through the lace curtains over the front windows Gerald could see children, dressed as ghosts, princesses and zombies, parading around the street.

Pumpkins, mutilated, yet smiling, sat on porches, gatekeepers to the underworld. People were laughing and frolicking, filling the children's baskets and bags with sugary junk, while others waited gleefully for the chance to open their doors to complete strangers.

*If only they knew,* Gerald thought. *If only they knew like I do what Halloween is really all about.*

The machine connected to Gerry's wheelchair beeped and it dragged his gaze away from the door.

"Damn it!" he said, his voice hoarse from the bout of coughing. The syringe driver needed to be refilled and if it wasn't refilled then things would get a whole lot worse for Gerald. Pain would set in like a thousand glass shards in his chest; pain so debilitating he might just relent and let it through the door.

He checked his watch again—5.44pm.

"Where the hell is she?" he said to the empty room. He scanned the door again and hoped she showed—before *it* did.

Doreen was his visiting nurse. Every second day she came to check his morphine driver, change his oxygen canister, take his blood pressure, listen to his chest, without fail. Doreen was the only other constant he could rely upon turning up at his front door. So where was she? Tonight, of all nights, she was late.

With some effort, Gerald wheeled himself over to the television table and retrieved the cordless phone. He had to find out where Doreen was. She had to get here so she could do all her stupid checks before it came. He'd dialled two numbers when there was a knock at the front door. He jumped in fright and the phone fell to the floor. His old heart beat out a staccato rhythm.

"No—not now," he whispered.

The shape of the figure on the other side of the front door was blurred by the frosted glass. Gerry wheeled himself behind the lounge chair and examined the silhouette. It was too tall to be *it*.

"Hello—Mr. Forsyth?" the visitor said.

Gerald didn't recognize the voice. "Who is it?" he said. "If you're trick-or-treating, I ain't interested."

There was a laugh; a woman's giggle. "No, no—I'm from Pastoral Care. Doreen sent me."

The old man frowned, concerned. "Doreen—where is she?"

"Could you let me in? It's getting quite chilly out here," she said.

The idea of opening the door terrified Gerald, but there was no sign of *it*, so if he moved quickly, opened the door and got it shut again, he would still be safe. Gerald wheeled up to the door, pulled the bolt back and opened the door until the chain latch caught. Through the gap he saw a fresh-faced brunette of about forty years of age smiling back at him.

"Hello," she said. "My name's Kelli. Kelli Pritchard."

Gerald saw the costumed children in the street behind her and shivered.

"Doreen sent you, you said?"

"That's right; she went home sick, so the manager asked me to check on you. So, can I come in?"

Gerald looked her up and down; she was attractive, he admitted, but he couldn't help but feel she was far too young to be a nurse. A gaggle of squealing laughter floated in from the street and the instinct to close the door reared over Gerald with the force of a tsunami.

"Come in! Come in!" he said, unlatching the chain in a flurry of hands and wheeling back to clear a path for her.

"Thanks so much," Kelli said. "It's nice to meet you, Mr. Forsyth." She held out her hand and after a moment, Gerald shook it.

"So, you're with Pastoral Care?" Gerald asked as he closed the door, resecured the chain and slipped the bolt firmly in place.

"I've been working there about a year now, actually," the nurse said, laying her handbag down on the lounge.

Gerald wheeled past her, back to his position directly in line with the front door, but far enough away so he couldn't be seen.

"Right," he said. "So, you should know how to change a syringe driver then?"

Kelli's face went blank and her jaw dropped; she stared at the machine and, right on cue, it beeped in alarm.

"Oh no," she said, putting her hand to her mouth. "I've never had to do that before."

Gerald's expression suddenly matched hers. "I beg your pardon?"

Instantly Kelli's face lit up with the widest smile. "Oh, Mr. Forsyth, of course I know how to change a driver—I've done it about a hundred times now!"

The old man's shock turned to scorn; he didn't like being made a fool of. "That's not funny," he said. "I should report you to your manager for a prank like that."

Kelli knelt down and started to open the lid of the driver. "You could do that if you like, but I'd wager Marci would tell you that you should just let me do my job."

Gerald's eyebrows rose, which only served to twist his mouth further. "Oh, you think so?"

Kelli flashed him that smile. "Come on Mr. Forsyth—I was just trying to have a little fun. That's what Halloween's all about."

He scoffed and stiffened in his wheelchair. The nurse frowned.

"Now what did I say wrong?" she said.

"Just hurry up and change the damn driver!"

Gerry glared at her; Kelli was appalled and she stood up, hands on her hips.

"Now Mr. Forsyth, there's no need to talk to me like that—I'm only trying to help you..."

"Well, if you want to help me, why don't you just do your damn job already and get going?"

"Mr. Forsyth, I don't appreciate your tone..."

"Stop patronizing me goddamn it and refill the driver!"

There was a heavy silence and Kelli looked away from him, instead kneeling again to work on the driver. Gerald knew he'd offended her, but he couldn't afford to get caught up in idle chit-chat and of course, she just had to be one of these new age kids who adored Halloween, didn't she? Naive, every one of them.

In a few minutes Kelli had changed the driver. Gerald noticed she'd done it a lot faster than Doreen would have, but then again, she was probably keen to get the job done and leave.

Good, he thought; the sooner the better.

"I have to take your blood pressure now," Kelli said. Her demeanor was flat now, clinical. Gerald lifted his arm and she wrapped the cuff around it, giving it a few vigorous pumps. "You're a little on the high side," she told him.

"Hmm," Gerald replied, his eyes back on the front door, thumbnail between his teeth.

Kelli removed the blood pressure cuff and put it away, then retrieved a stethoscope.

"Could you lift your shirt please?" He did so and she listened to his chest. "How's the coughing?" she asked.

"Not too bad."

"Any blood in the phlegm?"

Gerald shook his head and checked his watch—6.02pm, minutes from sundown. Kelli put the stethoscope away and then studied him. For a second their eyes locked, but they quickly turned their faces. In that moment he witnessed a determination in the nurse's expression.

"You know, just because you have emphysema doesn't mean you can boss people around," Kelli said suddenly.

"Excuse me?" Gerald said, taken aback.

Kelli packed her medical bag. "I'm here to help you, just like Doreen would if she were here. Sure, I'm a lot younger than her—and a lot younger than you—but that doesn't mean I can't do her job just as well."

"Really?" Gerald said, flustered; the girl had nous, he admitted.

"Yeah, and as a matter of fact I know everything Doreen does—because she trained me."

She folded her arms then, doubly proud of herself. The old man could see she had tons of that. He felt a smirk cross his lips, but he quickly concealed it with his hand.

"Did she?" he said.

"Yeah, she did. Is that okay with you?"

"Sure."

"Good."

Kelli gathered up the rest of her instruments into the bag and gave Gerald one last look. He knew she would have been thinking he was a son of a bitch, but he didn't care—he'd stopped making friends a very long time ago.

"Your oxygen is only half full so when I get back to the office, I'll arrange for a fresh one to be delivered tomorrow. Hopefully

Doreen will be back and she'll be able to take care of you. Try not to exert yourself too much and you should have enough oxygen until then."

Gerald sighed. "I know what to do with the cylinder."

Kelli nodded decisively. "Good," she said. "Well, if that's that then I'll be on my way."

Gerald could see she was just as stubborn as he could be; so be it, he wasn't about to apologize. "Goodbye," he said.

As Kelli turned and walked to the front door, a rumble of noise—a clamor of feet—rolled up Gerald's front porch.

"Oh look," Kelli cried. "Aren't they adorable?"

Gerald froze in his chair, unaware of how tightly he was gripping the arm rests.

"Oh no—what is it?"

Kelli's smile had returned. "Trick-or-treaters!"

"Don't open that door!" Gerald said. He saw confusion overwhelm the nurse's face.

"Sorry?"

"Get away from the door!"

Now Kelli wore a mask of disgust. "They're just kids—after some candy."

"I don't have any damn candy!"

Kelli waved him away. "Oh, I've got plenty in my bag—you always have to be prepared for Halloween I say…"

Gerald slammed his fist down on one of the arm rests. "There's no damn Halloween in my house!"

He saw disdain cross Kelli's features now, but he didn't care; this was his house—his rules.

"Well, it may be your house Mr. Forsyth, but I'm leaving and it's my candy." She put her hand on the door handle.

"No, don't—please!" Gerald said, his voice desperate. He gasped, but his breath was cut short; his saturated lungs suddenly refusing to work. His heart retaliated, initiating a beat that slammed it against his rib cage. Spots flashed before his eyes and a heavy darkness loomed.

"Mr. Forsyth?" he heard Kelli say.

"Tell them…tell them to run…" he murmured. "Tell…them

to stay away from Washington…and Blake!"

The last thing Gerald saw before the blackness swarmed inside his head was Kelli slamming the door on the trick-or-treaters and rushing toward him.

## 2

Old Gerald Forsyth's lungs sounded like a percolator in overload to Kelli, but it was his heart she was most concerned about.

Kelli surveyed the old man's face as she listened to his heart pound out 120 beats per minute. His skin was the color of a bedsheet and slick with a film of sweat. She hoped he would come out of unconsciousness soon; the last thing she needed was for a patient to deteriorate in her care. She couldn't afford to lose her job.

She shook her head, silently chastising herself. *Focus, god damn it—this man needs your help!* She retrieved her sphygnamometer and took another blood pressure reading. *Still high, but not dangerous.* She saw Gerald's telephone on the TV table and was about to reach for it and call 9-1-1 when her patient suddenly came to.

"Run!" he said, his eyes wild and jittery.

"Mr. Forsyth—can you hear me? It's Kelli."

"What?" his eyes locked on the nurse and widened further.

"You fainted," she said. "Do you remember?"

Kelli watched Gerald press the palm of his hand against his chest.

"Are you having chest pain?" she said, but the old man shook his head lazily.

"No…just…hard to breathe."

Kelli grabbed the oxygen mask and placed it over his face. "Okay, just take some slow, deep breaths for me—that's it. That's good."

She watched Gerald suck in air for several minutes and his blood pressure began to improve. His complexion, however, was still the characteristic paleness of someone with emphysema. Kelli breathed her own sigh of relief when Gerald's pulse dropped to ninety.

"Good—you're getting much better now," she said. "Now,

are you sure you're not having chest pain?"

Gerry nodded. "Yes..." his voice was lost within the oxygen mask.

"I should call a paramedic, just to be sure."

The old man squeezed her arm. "No—I said I'm fine."

Kelli frowned; Gerald's attack was so sudden, but she knew emphysema could be unpredictable, immobilizing a patient's breathing without warning. Yet she remembered how anxious he appeared just before his breathing failed him. There were trick-or-treaters at the door.

"So, what brought all that on?" she said.

He shrugged. "I...uh...don't know."

"You know those kids are gone now—you told them to run away."

She watched him crane his neck past her shoulder. "Good." He huffed.

"You don't like kids?"

The old man's bushy eyebrows rose and then knotted together. He sighed and a great plume of moisture obscured the downward turn of his mouth.

"Did they rock your roof or something, Mr. Forsyth? You were pretty adamant about chasing them away."

When Gerald didn't answer, Kelli was annoyed, but equally intrigued. While he sat there, steadying his breathing, she studied the contents of the living room. There was a worn leather recliner, cracked at the corners and a small, unsophisticated, turn-dial television set. On the wall behind it was a painting of a sailboat on a calm sea, possibly painted by Gerald himself. To the left of that wall was a broad teak display cabinet, filled with faded china plates, crystal drink glasses and tarnished silverware. The top of the cabinet was bare—not a single photograph or heirloom; nothing to indicate there had ever been anyone else in the house but Gerald Forsyth.

"How long have you lived alone, Mr. Forsyth?" Kelli said.

Gerald turned his gaze to her, startled. "This is my parents' house."

"So where are they?"

The bushy eyebrows rose. "They're dead—they died nearly thirty years ago."

"Hence my question: you live alone then?" She watched his eyes dart towards the front door.

"So what if I live alone?"

Kelli bit her lip. "No lady friend; no wife to cook you your meals, do your washing?"

Gerald plucked the oxygen mask from his face to reveal a grimace of aggravation. "No!" He wheeled away from her. "I think it's time for you to leave. I appreciate you attending to me, but I'm fine now—I don't need you here any longer."

Kelli sat down in one of the recliners and interlaced her fingers in her lap. "I can't leave; you just experienced difficulties with your breathing and unless you want me to call a paramedic, then I need to stay and make sure you don't have another attack."

"Why don't you just leave me alone!?" Gerry said, spittle falling to his chin.

Kelli leaned forward in the chair and held out her hands in mock surrender. "Mr. Forsyth, I'm only trying to work out what got you all so worked up—worked up enough to faint."

The old man shook with rage; Kelli had to be careful not to incite another attack. She knew she had no business meddling in this man's life, but she could see something painful kept him trapped, even more than the disease invading his body—something was eating away at his soul.

"I mean, one minute you're telling me to chase those kids away and the next thing you're suffocating," she continued. "What was so bad about those kids?"

Gerald's mouth became a thin line, but it did little to dampen his rage. "Get out."

Kelli shook her head. "Sorry, no can do. I'm a nurse and you're my patient; besides we're just having a chat."

"I don't want to talk—not to you—not to anyone!"

She watched his eyes return to the door. He was studying it with a passion and Kelli imagined he probably knew every grain of wood, every speck of corrosion on the brass handle.

"So given you don't like having kids around I take it you

don't have any of your own?"

Gerald's sideways glance could have turned her to stone. "No wife—remember?"

"Hey, that doesn't stop some people!" she said with a snigger. "Look at me—I'm a single mom with a 17-year-old son who spends more time talking to his Facebook friends than me."

"Hmpf," Gerald said with a slight chuckle of his own; Kelli was starting to chip away at his resolve. Yet, she still couldn't pull his gaze away from that door.

"You're waiting for something, aren't you?"

Gerald flinched this time and he looked to her, lips parted in surprise; he looked like a child caught with their hand in the cookie jar.

"What?" he muttered.

"Is someone coming to visit today—for Halloween, I mean; a relative or friend?"

"No."

"Then why do you keep staring at that damn front door?"

Gerald gripped the hand rims of the wheelchair and spun himself away from her towards the kitchen with a grunt of exertion.

"It's none of your damn business, okay!" he said.

Kelli's curiosity burned. She knew it often got the better of her, but it was one of the reasons she'd become a nurse. She thought talking to a patient could be just as effective, if not more effective, as administering medicine. She got up and followed him into the kitchen.

"Okay, look, I'm sorry," she said. "I know I can be a bit bull-headed and you're right, it is none of my business."

"You got that right," Gerald growled.

Kelli held out her hand for the old man to shake. "So, no hard feelings then?"

She watched Gerry look at her hand as if it were diseased. A moment passed before he sighed and quickly reached out to shake it and let it go.

"Great," Kelli said and went back into the living room to retrieve her bag. "If it's okay with you Mr. Forsyth, I'll get one of the night nurses to give you a call later on in the evening, just to make sure you're all right."

"Fine, whatever," he said, waving her away.

Kelli gathered her nurse's bag, willing herself to go out the front door; to shut up and leave the poor old man alone. She asked herself whether she should take his blood pressure one last time, listen to his lungs, but she knew she'd already overstayed her welcome.

"Okay then—I'll just say that the pleasure's been all mine then?"

Gerald didn't reply, only pulled the oxygen mask back over his face and concentrated on his breathing. Kelli went to the door and began to turn the door handle when an epiphany slapped her in the face. Smirking, she walked back into the living room to face him.

"Aren't you supposed to be leaving?" he snarled.

"You know, for someone who apparently hates kids, you're paying a lot of attention to all those trick-or-treaters walking about out there."

Gerry pulled his mask down in exasperation. He moved to speak, but hesitation crept in and he simply replaced his mask. Kelli was the one to wave her hand dismissively at him then. She turned for the door again.

"No, you're right—none of my business. Goodbye Mr. Forsyth."

As she reached for the handle, she heard Gerry take in a sharp breath. She turned to see his face was stark white, his eyes bulging and locked on the door behind her.

*Oh, no, not again.*

"What's wrong?" Kelli said.

A voice in her head told her to get away from the door; that it presented an immediate danger. Instinct simultaneously told her to run and stay still, yet her heart had already broken into a sprint. Beneath that desire to live however, was the even more powerful need to know.

There was a rap-rap-rap at the door.

Kelli jumped at the noise and whirled back to face the door. Through the dirty glass view-panel, she could make out the silhouette of a child standing on the other side.

"Oh, gosh—you scared me!" she said.

The child, a boy, from what she could tell, stood bolt upright, like a statue. Kelli could make out the faint outline of the costume he was wearing; some sort of enlarged headpiece or mask and a tattered suit jacket and trousers.

"It's just another trick-or-treater," Kelli said, smiling with relief.

She turned to Gerald and the smile was wiped from her face. The old man was trembling in his chair, his head shaking from side to side in denial. He gazed, unblinking at the boy and those eyes exuded fear.

"Mr. Forsyth?" Was he having another attack? No, this was something far worse; his entire body was infected with terror.

"Don't!" he said, and sucked in a new breath.

"Don't what—it's only a boy." She moved to open the door.

"No!"

Kelli rifled inside her handbag. "I'm just going to give him some candy, okay, and send him on his way."

"NO!"

Gerald tried to stand, as if to stop her, but her hand was already turning the doorknob and pulling the door wide open. The little boy—about ten years of age, she surmised—never shifted or acknowledged her. He simply looked straight ahead—at Gerald Forsyth.

"Hi there," Kelli said, but still the boy played statues.

The boy was short for his age, Kelli thought, but with the door open she could now get a better look at his costume. He wore a large Frankenstein headpiece—complete with rusty-looking rubber bolts at the temples—which made him appear a foot taller. Kelli gazed in wonder at his makeup, a rough mixture of putrescent greens and purples to capture an accurate depiction of a creature composed entirely of reanimated flesh. The suit he wore was charcoal grey, with some brown-colored stains on the lapel, elbows and knees.

"Oh my—I love your costume!" she said.

The boy's large black boots were neatly side by side, jutting against the threshold. Kelli crouched down to smile at him; the boy's pale grey eyes looked dead ahead. She followed his eyeline and found Gerald at the end of it, still trembling and paralyzed with fear.

*Why on earth would a grown man be afraid of a little boy?*

"Aren't you going to say hello Mr. Forsyth?"

"Get…get away!" he said, through gritted teeth.

Kelli stood and thrust her hands on her hips. "Oh, this is getting ridiculous! What is it with you and Halloween? It's just harmless fun!"

Gerald shook his head and she sighed and held out a packet of pumpkinhead caramels to the boy.

"Here's your candy," Kelli said. "Why don't you come in so we can get a better look at your amazing costume?"

"Stop—no!" Gerald wailed, holding out his trembling right hand.

Kelli was truly annoyed with the old man's attitude now. She'd tried in vain to get him to open up about it and he refused; he was just a grumpy old man griping at the younger generation. Ironically, Gerald Forsyth was behaving just like the thing he so despised.

"I'm sorry Mr. Forsyth, but this is my candy and I'm going to give it to him."

Kelli heard the door close and the double clip-clop sound of shoes on the floorboards.

"Good boy," Kelli said, returning her attention to the boy. "Here you go." She frowned when he didn't take the candy. "You don't want them?"

The little Frankenstein kept up his staring contest with Gerry.

"You're a quiet one, aren't you? Well, here you go then." She tucked the packet into the breast pocket of the boy's jacket. She smoothed down the shoulders of the jacket and picked off a piece of dirt. "This your first trick or treat then?" She chuckled. "I remember my first time too. I was so nervous, but I had a group of friends to go with. She glanced at the front porch. "No one came with you though, huh?"

Franken-boy and Gerald's gazes were locked on and Kelli wondered if either of them had blinked. She reached out and gently took hold of his chin and turned his face to her.

"Hey, what's your name, sweetie?"

Strangely, the boy's eyes remained facing the old man and his skin felt ice cold.

"You're freezing!" she said, retracting her hand away.

Gerald suddenly wheeled forward, his finger outstretched. "Get out of my house!" he shrieked.

Kelli tutted. "Come on—we'd better leave Mr. Forsyth in peace." She gripped the boy's shoulder to lead him out, but he wouldn't budge. When she tried to open the door, the knob wouldn't move either. "Oh, I must have turned the lock when I closed it—silly me."

Gerald began to sob. He sank his face into his hands.

"No, no, no, no, no…"

"The lock's stuck," Kelli said, flabbergasted. A twinge of panic began to creep into her chest. She looked at the boy looking at Gerald. He hadn't moved in so long; hadn't even blinked. She glanced at his nostrils and chest.

*Is he even breathing?*

She yanked on the door, but it didn't even rattle. "Mr. Forsyth, the door won't open."

The old man began to scream, his voice hoarse and ragged, like he was choking on a hundred marbles. The boy seemed unperturbed by the fact the old man suddenly seemed to be suffocating.

"Did you lock the door?" she asked the boy.

Then the child Frankenstein turned to look at her, as if noticing her for the first time. Kelli glimpsed something dark and hungry in his eyes, something that wanted to drink in her fear. As she tried to fathom what was happening, a trickle of blood suddenly erupted from the boy's left nostril, all over his jacket.

"Oh, my God—your nose!"

The trickle became a flood, as a torrent of dark blood escaped both nostrils, spilling violently all down the front of his costume, spattering his shoes and pooling on the floor. Kelli jumped out of the spray and instantly reached for the tissues in her bag.

"Oh, my Lord!"

She reached out with the tissues to pinch the boy's nose, but before she could he opened his mouth impossibly wide and released a great regurgitation of blood all over her arm. The geyser of blood that hit the floor was far too much for a ten-year-old boy to sustain. When the Frankenstein child smiled widely at her through oozing red lips and looked down at the floor to admire the mess he'd made, Kelli screamed.

## 3

The blood poured from the boy's nose as if it were a leaky faucet. Kelli sat on the floor near Gerald gawking in horror at the steady drip-drip-drip. The bleeding had a hypnotic effect and she found her eyes tracking each drop's descent from nose to floor. A great pool of blood was spreading out from where the boy stood, the rug on the floor sucking the foul liquid up like a sponge.

The boy was watching both her and Gerald now. His eyes were devoid of color and were so, so cold. Perhaps it was from the blood loss, Kelli wondered. But it didn't make sense; with all that bleeding the boy should have been dead—certainly not conscious. For the first time, the nurse didn't know what to think, or what to say. There was only the boy's blood and his eyes and she believed she might quite possibly drown in both of them. She would have too if Gerald's croaked voice didn't suddenly drag her out of the trance.

"We have move away from him."

Kelli reluctantly turned her gaze from the boy to the old man. Her throat was dry and when she swallowed it made a clicking sound.

"He's…he's bleeding," she said.

"I know—now stay back from him!" Gerald replied and he seemed to have suddenly become concerned for her wellbeing rather than his own.

Kelli felt the crawl of confusion begin to mingle with the fear which had already seeded in her mind. The nurse in her demanded she go to the boy's aid, but common sense screamed at her to do as Gerald commanded. She looked at him; there was still terror in his creased features, but she could tell this was a terror all too familiar.

"Who is he?" she asked him.

Gerald shook his head. Kelli turned from him and faced the boy.

"Who are you?"

The boy's dull eyes shifted to her almost instantly.

"Don't talk to him!" Gerald cried, gripping her by the shoulder.

Kelli ignored the old man and watched a long string of sticky blood ooze from his nose and down his chin.

"Do you… realize you're bleeding?"

The Franken-child stared at her and smiled once more, blood turned his tiny yellow teeth pink. The boy stuck out his tongue and lapped at it. It was the only part of him that moved; no blinking, no turn of the head. He was a bleeding statue that was anything but miraculous.

"Do you live around here?" Kelli said, lifting herself into a crouch. "Do your parents know you're here?"

"For god's sake stop it woman!" Gerald implored.

Kelli watched his smile vanish and his eyes flick to the old man. There was a definite glint of ferocity in those vacant eyes. More blood flowed out too, as if in response to the old man's voice. Kelli turned to the old man.

"You know who this boy is, don't you?"

"Don't!" Tears pooled in his eyes.

"I need to know who he is—I have to help him."

"There's nothing you can do for him!"

A noise emanated from behind her and Kelli turned back to see the boy's mouth was wide open. The guttural echo resounded from deep within the boy's throat; a prolonged moan that resembled a child in a choir chanting—chanting from inside a cave. As she tried to comprehend the sound, the boy took a step towards them and hissed, a spray of bloody saliva pluming in the air.

"Get up!" Gerald ordered, pulling Kelli away.

"What is he doing?"

"Move back!"

The boy took another step and Kelli noticed that it was more a shamble, as if he was in fact a miniature version of Mary Shelley's famous monstrosity. Kelli wondered if the boy was simply putting on an act; that somewhere under his costume there were bags of fake blood with tubes connected to his nose. Could this boy conceive of such a cruel prank?

Kelli felt a significant amount of strength in Gerald's grip as he twisted her around and thrust her towards the kitchen. She staggered forward, but looked back over her shoulder to see her would-be rescuer rising out of his chair to his feet. He blocked the boy's path with outstretched hands.

"Stop!" he told the boy.

The child stopped and cocked his head at the old man like a dog trying to compute a master's command. Kelli saw Gerald shudder, as he struggled to stay upright. A combination of muscle weakness and fear, she imagined. She was paralyzed as well, both in mind and body. What was occurring in Gerald Forsyth's home should have been a joke, a child's idea of giving an old man a scare on Halloween, but the blood looked so real and the boy looked as if he was—

"Is he—?"

Gerald's hands became fists. "Shut up! Shut up you stupid woman or you'll attract his attention!"

Kelli swallowed and watched the two of them. There was history between the old man and the boy; something dark and terrible. For a moment she wondered if Gerald had done something to this boy, that maybe the old man's gruff exterior covered a past, unthinkable sin.

"You tell me who he is!" Kelli said.

This time Gerald whirled on her. "Listen to me! Just shut up and listen!"

Kelli flinched, but the boy simply watched and listened.

"You have to get out of here!" the old man said.

"How?"

"The back door, it's off the kitchen! Go now goddamn it!"

Kelli looked to her right and she saw, past the kitchen bench, was the back door. She looked back to Gerry, uncertainty festering in the pit of her stomach. She looked into Gerald's eyes and saw the sadness and guilt residing there and she realized he was trying to save her. For the first time she felt truly sorry for him, but her sympathy was short-lived when the bleeding boy suddenly reached out to grab Gerald's wrists.

She shrieked as the two of them struggled. Despite the constant flow of blood, and his deathly appearance, the boy was impossibly strong. Gerald dropped to his knees and the boy shifted his hands to grip his throat. The boy smiled in delight as his captive began to suffocate. It was at this moment something inside Kelli snapped.

It happened so quickly that she couldn't remember herself moving. She simply found herself standing beside the boy and with one hand, shoving him off her patient. As the boy toppled into the TV table, Kelli reached down and lifted the gasping Gerry to his feet, placed him in the wheelchair and wheeled him out of the kitchen. The rubber tread left black marks on the floorboards.

"Is the back door unlocked?" she cried at Gerald, but the old man was hunched over.

Kelli steered past the kitchen bench, past the 1980s Formica cupboards and small sink towards the door. Panting with exertion she glanced over her shoulder—*no sign of the boy*. She reached down and tried to turn the handle as fear burned in her throat.

"It's locked!"

She scanned the wall beside the door for a key hook, but there was none.

*Even if there was a key, Kelli, was it Gerald who locked the door or had it been the boy? How could he lock the entire house if he hadn't been in the house before, stupid!*

She gently shook Gerald's shoulder and pressed her fingers to his throat to feel the steady thrum of his pulse.

"Mr. Forsyth—wake up!"

Gerald stirred and coughed, gasping for air; Kelli quickly put the oxygen mask over his face.

"Gerald—is there a key for the back door?"

Fear filled the old man with alertness and he began to fish around frantically in his pockets. Kelli watched him stare at the edge of the wall separating the kitchen from the living room as he searched; she looked to the same spot, dreading what might emerge there. The old man almost jumped up from his wheelchair when he finally found the key. He pushed it into Kelli's palm and she tried it in the keyhole.

"It won't turn!" she said.

"No, that's impossible." Gerald turned in his chair to reach back and turn the key with his gnarled hands. He grunted and strained to unlock the door, but it wouldn't budge.

"Goddamn it!" he said.

Kelli wrapped her own hands around his and twisted, but not even their combined strength could unlock the door.

"It's no good," she said.

They looked at each other, tears in each other's eyes; an equal sense of hopelessness. The moment was lost, however, when they both realized neither of them had been watching the wall. A shuffling noise wrenched their gazes back to that awful spot.

The boy staggered into the kitchen area from the other side of the wall. His nose still trickled blood and his entire front was now covered in a thick red tar. Droplets fell to the floor like deformed rubies, exploding on the linoleum floor to be smeared beneath the child's lethargic footsteps.

Kelli screamed; there was simply no reason for what she was seeing. The boy was coming for them and intended to kill them both. The reason why hardly mattered anymore. She just needed to escape.

"What are we going to do?" her voice broke in fear.

Gerald had again been left paralyzed by the boy's horrifying march, so she reached down and shook his shoulders.

"Mr. Forsyth!"

He shuddered and blinked, his eyes locked on hers. A moment passed, until his eyes widened in recognition. He reached past her and pointed to the hallway just off the kitchen.

"The bathroom!" he said. "Go!"

Kelli followed his pointing finger and nodded in acknowledgement. Quickly, she pushed him through it just as the bleeding boy came within a few feet of them. The child hissed as they made their escape. Despite Kelli's speed, the boy was relentless and immediately gave chase, one shambling footstep at a time.

"Hurry!" Gerald cried, and his pleas pushed Kelli into a panic. In her haste to get them across the hall into the bathroom, the wheels of the old man's chair twisted and almost toppled the chair over. Kelli summoned one last ounce of strength and managed to keep the chair upright and pushed it through the door.

"Close the door!" Gerald said. Kelli left the safety of the chair and hurried to the door. As she pulled it closed, she saw the terrifying child advancing. She slammed the door closed in the boy's bleeding face.

"Now put something against it—we need to keep him out," he told her.

Kelli grabbed the fortunately overflowing cane laundry basket and thrust it in front of the door. A moment later the door shook under the weight of a great pounding.

"Don't let it in!"

Kelli leant her back into the door. Her body jerked and rocked under the impossible power of the boy's urgent thrusting. How the boy had so much strength, yet little movement, Kelli had no inkling. From the terror in Gerald's eyes, she knew there was a little a door could do against such a horror. She watched the old man run his hands through the few strands of hair left on his pate.

"Oh, God, please—make it go away!" he sobbed.

The door boomed again and almost came open. Kelli shrieked and slammed her shoulder into it. The boy's cold, alabaster fingers crept through the gap and clawed at the air, as if tasting the fear in the room.

"No—get out!" Kelli said.

"Move out of the way!" When the nurse looked to Gerald, she saw him frenetically wheel his chair backwards in the direction of the door. She moved out of the way as the chair crashed into the door and forced it closed.

"Lock the wheels!" he said.

Kelli bent and clicked the wheel locks firmly into place. The boy, now unable to exert any pressure on the door, went into a frenzy of kicking and hissing, his fists like hammers on the wood. The door rattled with the resonance of a jackhammer on the back of Gerald's wheelchair, rocking the old man forward and back. Kelli saw tears roll down his weathered cheeks. He covered his ears to block out the child's wailing and it was several minutes before the tirade ceased. Eventually, a grave silence overwhelmed everything.

"He's stopped…gone!" Kelli said, smiling; she couldn't hide the relief on her face, but Gerald hadn't lost his somber expression.

"No, he's still there…" he muttered.

He gazed up at her then and Kelli could tell by his gaunt face and sorrowful eyes, that he was speaking the truth.

"…and he'll never leave without me."

## 4

Gerald wanted it all to disappear: the boy, Kelli, his emphysema, the whole goddamned world. But he knew that wish, his one hope, would never be fulfilled. Not without one significant sacrifice.

He wasn't certain how long he'd been crying, sitting in a miserable heap in his wheelchair. He didn't know how long Kelli had been trying to talk to him. He only focused on the silence coming from the other side of the bathroom door; from the ever-patient demon he knew all too well.

Yet, this time was different; the boy was, for the very first time, inside his house. Gerald had never allowed that to happen before. It was the damned nurse's fault, he told himself. If only she'd never opened the door; if only his regular nurse Doreen, who was much better, quieter—and efficient—at her job, hadn't been sick, then none of this would ever have happened.

If only…if only he'd never decided to go trick-or-treating in a blizzard all those years ago.

Kelli's voice, taut with desperation, brought him out of his reverie.

"Mr. Forsyth—can you hear me? What are we going to do now?"

Gerald lifted his head to look at Kelli. Her eyes were wide and white, pupils dilated with terror and a glaze of sweat on her brow. The old man knew this experience would age her ten years.

"What is going on?" Kelli said, her voice quivering. "You know something about that boy—don't deny it."

He wiped the sweat from his top lip with the back of his hand. "We need…" he began, "…to be very quiet."

"Who is he?" Kelli cried, pointing an accusing finger at the door.

Gerald took a deep calming breath, but instead of providing life-giving oxygen, his chest pressed in on him like a giant vice. He squeezed his eyes closed and tried to ignore the fact that soon his need for oxygen would overwhelm everything.

"Just…just a kid."

"'Just a kid'—what sort of kid walks through your house, bleeds…pint after pint…of blood all over your floor and tries to choke you to death?"

The old man scowled. "You let it in."

Kelli recoiled and looked away from him. He watched her swallow down the guilt. Yet she didn't avert her gaze from him for long, her inquisitive green eyes burrowing into his.

"Why do you refer to the boy as 'it' or 'a kid' when you know very well who he is?"

"Please…be quiet."

She grabbed him by his shoulders and shook him. "No—you need to tell me who that boy is and what he wants with you!"

The old man slapped his hand down on the arm of his wheelchair. "Shut up! Just shut up!" Your stupidity allowed him to get into my house and now I have no idea how to get him out!"

Kelli winced, feeling the sting of the stupid comment again, yet in his rage, Gerald had also begun to open up about his knowledge of the boy.

"You said 'him'."

"For god's sake, will you be quiet?"

Kelli sighed and reached into her coat to retrieve her cell phone.

"Wait—what are you doing?" Gerald said.

"I'm calling the police!" She began to dial 9-1-1.

"No! You can't!" He reached for her, but Kelli turned her back and put the phone to her ear.

"Please, don't call the police!" he said behind her, his voice cracking.

Kelli turned back to face him and pulled the phone away from her ear. "Then tell me why! We need to get the police here to help us."

The bathroom door shuddered with a terrifying jolt and the pair froze. The thing—the boy—on the other side was still there. Gerald knew it was listening in, biding its time; savoring the fear escalating between him and the nurse. This was what it wanted—to induce terror in their hearts.

The old man looked at Kelli holding the phone in her hand; she was shaking. From where he sat, he could hear the 9-1-1 dispatcher calling out for someone to respond.

"9-1-1—what's your emergency?"

"Hang up the phone Kelli," Gerald told her as gently as possible.

Kelli looked at the phone in her palm and suddenly realized what she'd been doing. She raised the phone to her ear.

"Don't!" he begged.

Kelli's eyes flared at him with disdain as she spoke to the dispatcher.

"Hello? This is Kelli Pritchard. I need help."

"Hang up the damn phone!"

BOOM. The door rocked against the old man's chair.

"I'm a nurse…from St Stephen's Hospice Care," Kelli said. "I'm at a patient's house …at Gerald Forsyth's house…and someone is trying to hurt us."

"What's your address, ma'am?" the dispatcher's voice came back.

"116 Bla—"

Gerald strained his arm to grab the phone from Kelli's hand, but he didn't hold onto it for long. Before the nurse could object—and finish telling the dispatcher his address—he threw the phone hard into the bathtub where it smashed into half a dozen pieces, the back cover, battery and plastic screen sliding around the inside of the tub to settle near the plughole.

"Why the hell did you do that!?" Kelli said.

Gerald watched her try to salvage the phone from the tub and wondered the same thing. Had all these years of terror finally sent him mad? Even if he were, he couldn't risk having the police come to his aid. Who knows what it might do if it were cornered. Its…*capabilities* were essentially limitless. If he could just keep it at bay until dawn then it would be gone…at least for one more year. He checked his watch. It was almost 8pm.

"What is wrong with you?" Kelli said, and when she looked at him her eyes were reddened with hot tears.

"You need to listen to me now," Gerald said, trying not to look her directly in the eyes.

"Listen to you! What are you going to say that will be of any use to me? Unless you're willing to tell me who that boy is and what the hell he wants, then I don't want to hear a single word from you. You got that, old man?!"

Silence filled the room for several moments as Gerald battled with guilt and fear. Kelli chose to sit on the floor and lean against the bathtub, exhausted no doubt from the adrenaline rushing around her blood. Gerald studied her and found himself admiring her courage and determination—perhaps not so much her disrespect for her elders, but her "take-no-crap" attitude was, he admitted, endearing. He wanted to trust her with his secret, but he didn't know where to begin.

"My son is going to be wondering where I am," Kelli said suddenly.

"I thought you said your son hardly spoke to you."

"What I meant was he'll be wondering where I am when he comes home and finds there's no dinner," Kelli chuckled.

"Oh, I see." Gerald felt a release of the tension in the room. "What's your boy's name?"

"Adam."

"That's a good name."

"Thanks," Kelli said, but Gerald saw that uncomfortableness surfacing on her face again.

"So, no one else at home—no father, boyfriend?" Gerald asked.

Kelli chuckled derisively. "No, I kicked his ass out years ago, unfaithful S-O-B."

"Ah—but forgive me, I didn't mean to pry."

Kelli waved a hand to dismiss him. "No, no it's fine—looks like we'll be spending the night together, so we might as well get cozy, right?"

Kelli smiled and Gerald smiled back; it would take time, but the old man felt that the two of them could get along if they put their minds to it. The nurse looked to the bathroom door again, a worried expression returning to her face.

"So, what about this boy then, Gerald—what's his name?"

The old man felt his shoulders sag and a heavy, grating sigh pass his lips. He closed his eyes, so tired, so eager for rest. Tears rolled down his cheeks, dragging him down into the abyss of despair that kept him breathless, kept him in his chair.

"It's…a very long story," he replied.

Kelli got to her knees to crawl over to him. Gingerly she rested her hand on his.

"I'm willing to hear it, if you're willing to tell it," she said.

Gerald saw sincerity—and trust—in the nurse's eyes. She smiled and he found himself smirking.

"It's from when I was…a boy."

Kelli looked from him to the door; no doubt she was thinking of the boy on the other side. She would be putting two and two together; he certainly hoped so, because it would make the telling much easier.

"So, a long time ago then?" she said.

Gerald nodded and exhaled a long, wavering, tremulous release. He tried to think of the words to choose. He hated talking, preferring the confines of his own head, but there was no turning back now. He'd already given birth to the secret and now he had to nurture it. Perhaps, by letting it free, he would finally free himself. When he looked up, he found Kelli staring at him, waiting desperately.

"Would you mind—I mean, just to help me out a little—tell me a little about your childhood?" he asked.

Kelli's eyes widened. "I thought you were going to tell me your story?"

"I will, I will—I'm just trying to…talk."

"I thought we needed to stay quiet?"

"Just...keep your voice low and I think we'll be fine."

Kelli's brow softened. "Okay...if it helps." She rubbed her palms on her knees and Gerry understood she felt anxious, given all she'd witnessed so far this evening.

"I don't know where to start," she said with a nervous laugh.

The irony wasn't lost on Gerald, but if she could just show him courage then he might be able to use it. He reached out and patted her hand.

"Tell me where you grew up," he said.

"Iowa—Des Moines."

"You were born there?"

"Yeah—I was the youngest of three. I've got two older brothers."

Gerald raised an eyebrow. "That must have made for an interesting household—all that testosterone flying around."

Kelli nodded, the memories making her smile. "Oh, yeah, but my mom raised us pretty sternly—single-handedly, too, after my dad injured his back in a work accident. He'd just gotten back from Vietnam when it happened. Turned out he had a piece of shrapnel in his back he didn't even know was there. One day he just bent over and it severed a nerve or something. He could barely move his legs after that; spent most of his time in bed. Lucky for us the Veterans' pay checks came through fairly regular so Mom could keep paying the bills and putting food in our bellies."

Gerald rubbed his chin. "That must have been hard for your mother?"

"It was, but she had resolve. She made sure we went to school every day. After a while Mom managed to get a job at the town library and Dad wasn't completely useless. If anything, he had plenty of time to talk to us, teach us with words rather than actions. It helped take the focus away from his back pain."

"Sounds like you all worked well together," Gerald said.

"We did, but Mom was the glue, you know, a real organizer."

"A fine woman—is she still alive?"

Kelli shook her head. "No, she died about five years ago now. Dad died in 1982; heart attack."

"Sorry to hear that." Gerald hesitated, talk of death softening the conversation, but he knew he had to keep going. "How about school—did you like school?"

"Oh, yeah—I was pretty good at everything—except algebra." A wry smirk wrinkled her nose. "Why does this sound like a counselling session?"

Gerald smiled. "Well, if it is, it's doing me a world of good. Let's just say that by you telling me your story, it might go some way to helping you understand mine when I tell it to you."

Kelli nodded. "So, you want me to keep going?"

"Please. Tell me about your friends. Did you have a bunch of friends to play with?"

She laughed and Gerald could tell she was invoking a very fond memory. She was calming down, which in turn was keeping his anxiety at bay.

"Just one—Marcia Hoffman," Kelli said, staring off into the past. "She was such a tiny thing, all dark hair and freckles. She was always so bright and joyful, that girl."

"You spent a lot of time together?"

"We were inseparable; both our families were. We went everywhere together: fishing trips in the summer, ski trips in the winter. It was almost as if we were an extended family. Marcia's parents were real close to mine and Marcia's dad used to help out with odd jobs around the house since Dad couldn't do them. Marci's Dad owned a corn farm and we used to spend hours running through the stalks playing hide and seek."

Gerald chuckled, but the visualization of the two girls running and playing only served to evoke memories of his own childhood. A childhood plagued with guilt and fear.

"The holidays were always so much fun; Halloween especially," Kelli continued, on a roll now. "It was a given in both households."

The old man picked at a hole in one of the arms of his wheelchair. "So you and Marcia would have done the whole trick-or-treating thing, then?"

"Oh, definitely—we always tried to out-dress each other. Marcia was into fairies and princesses, but it was witches and

Vampirella for me." She frowned. "I thought you hated the very mention of Halloween."

Gerald nodded, still staring at the hole. "I used to be just like you," he said. "Halloween was always something to look forward to."

"So, what happened?"

He pinched the bridge of his nose, trying to keep the pain of recollection at bay. He had to try and make the words come. He lifted his gaze to the nurse and tried to look into her, to find strength in the goodness of her soul.

"I had a friend once, just like your Marcia," he said.

"What was his name?"

"Donnie—Donald Psalter. We used to do everything together too, especially Halloween, but it was Halloween that tore us apart."

"How?"

Suddenly a low moan crept in beneath the bathroom door, like the sound of something dying. Kelli sat bolt upright.

"Oh, God—was that the boy?"

"Yes—he's crying," Gerald said.

"Crying—why would he be crying?"

Gerald looked right into Kelli's eyes. "Because he knows how the story ends."

## 5

Kelli was torn between the desire to have Gerald speak the truth and the trepidation of just what that "truth" might entail.

She studied the old man and tried to compose herself; she didn't want to trust him, but she had little choice. He'd destroyed her phone and now she was trapped with him. Worse still, a seemingly homicidal kid was lurking outside the bathroom door—and only Gerald knew why. She had her own notions about the connection between the old man and the boy and she feared that Gerald was about to prove her right. She forced a reassuring smile.

"Go ahead—you can tell me," she said.

Gerald scratched at his balding head and flashed his own, albeit nervous, smile back.

"Okay," he said, but then he held up a palm to placate her. "Now, whatever I tell you, no matter how crazy it might sound, you just need to listen. Okay?"

Kelli took a deep breath, trying not to point out all the different kinds of "crazy" she'd witnessed in the past few hours.

"Sure, I understand."

Gerald nodded and took a long deep breath.

"You okay?" Kelli said, continuing to play the part of caring nurse.

"Yes—I just wish I had a bit of Dutch courage," he said.

"You just take your time—start at the beginning."

Gerald licked his cracked lips. "Well, here goes, then. As I said before, I grew up right here in this house; born in '44, right smack bang in the middle of the war. My dad worked at the *Tribune*—in the printing press. Fortunately, the war meant there was plenty of despair to write about. My mother, God rest her soul, stayed at home with me. She was a wonderful woman, kind and forthright. My Pa was a very tall, strong man, but he had a soft side too. He liked to joke around and when he wasn't working, he always had time for me."

Kelli wanted to urge him on, but only to bring a quick closure to the madness and her fear.

"You said you were an only child?"

"Yes, my mother ended up getting a severe infection, which left her barren."

"Must have been hard for your family?"

Gerald nodded. "Sometimes, but my parents doted on me a lot so I was never really alone. And once I got to school, finding friends became a bit of a…well…no-brainer. There were a lot of kids like me back then—only children, I mean. Times were pretty tough and having too many mouths to feed during the war was fraught with danger. So, our schoolmates became like the brothers and sisters I couldn't have."

Kelli looked to the door. "He's…gone quiet."

She watched Gerald turn to stare at the door; she imagined he could see straight through the wood at the boy standing on the other side.

"He's listening," he said.

"Who is he?"

Gerald turned back to face her. "I'm getting to that." He interlaced his leathery fingers then and his knuckles turned the color of the first snow. To Kelli, it was as if he'd captured a memory in his palms and she wondered, if he opened them, whether the memory would fly away.

"Donald Psalter was his name," Gerald said, with a smirk. "I remember the day at school when he just came up to me and introduced himself. 'My name's Donnie—what's yours?' he said. He was so happy to see me, regardless of the fact that we were strangers. He must have been lonely too, I suppose. He had this cheeky grin, really mischievous—probably had something to do with the fact he had two or three teeth growing through crooked." Gerald chuckled to himself. "He had this tattered *Minnesota Twins* cap on his head, which was one size too small for him, so all his curly hair stuck out at the sides."

"I can picture him," Kelli said, and thought of what the Frankenstein child would have looked like—alive and well.

"He grabbed my right hand and just shook the blazes out of it," Gerald continued. "My arm felt like jelly for the rest of the day."

"What happened then?"

Gerald looked at her as if for the first time. "Oh, well, of course, I told him who I was and that was it—it was like 'Okay, now we're best friends.'"

Kelli laughed. "Just like that, huh?"

"From that day on, we did everything together; played ball in the park, rode our bicycles around the city, threw rocks at old houses—all the things little boys shouldn't be doing, you know?"

The old man began to tear up. "I remember this one time when we went to the county fair and Donnie, oh, he was a scamp—he stole this great big jar of toffees. We took them back to his house. We ate so many we were almost sick."

"Really?" Kelli said, smiling.

"Yeah—he was a lot of fun, that kid."

Kelli saw a wave of sorrow wipe the smile from the old man's face; she now knew how strong the bond between Gerald and Donnie had been. Still was.

"Inseparable," she said.

"In every way."

From the corner of her eye Kelli could see through the gap in the bottom of the door the boy's shadow move.

"So, is that who this is—Donnie?"

Gerald raised his eyes to her; he looked pale and lost. "Do you really want to know why I live alone, Miss Pritchard?

"I…I don't know."

"Have you ever been alone—I mean so alone that your only companion is the thoughts in your head?"

"We've all felt alone at some point—"

"No," Gerald interrupted. "No, you don't understand. Loneliness isn't about not having anyone else around—it's about… being alone…inside; being trapped inside your bad memories.

Kelli saw that Gerald's legs were shaking and when he spoke next his words almost failed him.

"Every Halloween…every goddamned Halloween…it comes… haunts me."

"The boy?"

Gerald nodded and his trembling made it look like he was gripped by a tremor. "It started so long ago. One day he…it…just showed up…on my doorstep; after so many years. I'd forgotten… then, there he was. I didn't know what to do. I panicked and slammed the door in its face and hid like a cowardly dog."

"When did this happen?" Kelli asked, swallowing hard.

"Not long after…after I was diagnosed with emphysema; was almost as if it knew. And for so long I've been able to keep it out and now it's here. It's waited years for this moment. It knows… it knows that I'm going to die!"

Kelli reached out and squeezed his dry hand. "You're not going to die—"

"I am, goddamn it! Oh, can't you see that!?"

Kelli released his hand, eager not to inherit his despair. She saw his eyes pleading to her, desperate for understanding. Deep down she knew what he was saying, but the notion was still unbelievable.

"But…he's just a boy," she said, but it was more to convince herself than anything else.

"He's not just a boy! It's Donnie for god's sake! You know that! And he's here—here for me!"

Kelli felt his panic threatening to overwhelm her. She retreated from the old man, sliding along the floor until her back slammed into the bathtub. She'd heard the truth and now she wanted to flee from it.

"But it's just a kid—it can't be Donnie!" she cried.

"Believe me—it is!"

"What happened to him?"

Gerald clawed at his face in frustration, drew blood from the bridge of his nose. He was mad—with grief.

"He died! He died…because of me!"

Gerald's grief flowed out in his tears, like his secret had left his soul raw and bleeding.

Kelli watched the old man shake with sorrow, listened to it catch in his useless lungs. Anguish in all its hideous beauty, bringing a man down to the same level as a child. There was a child at the door—a dead child; a ghost child. Returned from the grave on Halloween to wreak what—vengeance—a message? Whatever it sought to do, Kelli knew Gerald didn't want it, she could see that as plain as day.

As she looked at him a question she didn't want to ask parted her lips.

"Did…did you kill him?" she said.

Gerald lifted his head from his hands, a grimace expanding his moist cheeks.

"He died…because of me."

"What happened to Donnie?" Kelli whispered, and her eyes moved to the door; the boy's shadow was gone.

Gerald wiped the tears from his face with his palms, sniffed back the sadness and swallowed it down.

"I've kept it a secret…for so long."

"Maybe it's time you let that secret out," Kelli said, and she wasn't making a suggestion.

The old man motioned to reply, but a knock at the bathroom door froze them. The skin of Kelli's arm erupted with gooseflesh and rode the wave up her spine to the fear center of her brain.

"It's the boy!" she gasped.

Gerald looked over his shoulder, his face contorting with terror. "I don't know if I can face him!"

Kelli went to him and touched his arm. "I think…I think this is what he wants; for you to tell his story."

"I can't!" Gerald cried.

"Tell me, Gerald—tell me his story."

Kelli clasped her hands around his and smiled reassuringly. Through the door they heard Donnie knocking and Gerald knew it was time to open the door to his past and set it free.

## 6

Duluth, Minnesota, October 31, 1952

The roar of the wind rattled the windows, rousing Gerald Forsyth from his sleep. Exhilaration surged through his little body, like a switch had been turned on inside him. He threw the blankets off himself, seemingly ignorant to the biting cold, bounded over to his dresser and opened the top drawer. His hands rummaged through the piles of comic books and baseball cards within until he found what he was looking for. He switched on the walkie talkie and put it to his lips; it only barely covered the smile on his face.

"Donnie? Donnie?" he said and released the talk button. A hiss of static, heightened by the brewing storm outside, was the only reply. "Donnie? It's Gerry! Pick up—over!"

The static was abruptly cut by a soft rustling.

"Yeah?" came a weary voice.

Gerald bounced on the spot. "It's here!" he said. "Today's the day—over."

"What?" Donnie replied and Gerald sighed at his friend's

inability to rouse in the morning.

"Halloween—it's Halloween you doofus!"

Another moment's pause, then: "It is?"

"Check your calendar—it's October 31! Yesterday was October 30, remember?"

Gerald listened as he heard Donnie stumble about inside his bedroom; he must have left the button on his walkie talkie on. Gerald shook his head at his friend's forgetfulness. He opened his mouth to chide Donnie about it when he realized he wouldn't hear him anyway. He tossed his walkie talkie on the bed and ran to his window, pulling it open. A wall of freezing air slapped Gerald in the face. The world was painted in grey, but Gerald ignored the oncoming storm and instead stretched his head outside to peer at the top floor window of the house next door, the window of Donnie Psalter's bedroom.

"Hey doofus!" Gerald yelled above the wind. "You've still got your button down!"

A pale-faced boy with a scruffy bowl haircut appeared at his own window. Donnie opened the window and instantly regretted it, wrapping his arms around himself in a wasted bid to protect himself from the cold.

"What?" Donnie cried back, the gale catching his voice and blasting it miles into town.

"You've left your button—oh forget it! We can hear each other now anyways." Gerald said, but then he reconsidered the sky. "Pretty much..."

Suddenly the window on the bottom floor of Donnie's house slid open fiercely and the disgruntled visage of Margaret Psalter—Donnie's mother—appeared. She cast both boys a look significantly icier than the blizzard about to bear down on Duluth.

"I can hear both of you!" she said.

"Sorry, Mom!" Donnie replied, shrinking back from the window.

"Sorry Mrs. Psalter," Gerald added.

"Get inside the pair of you, before you freeze to death."

Gerald's mother Bethany wouldn't let her son go outside with the blizzard, but she knew by his jittery excitement that she was going to have a lot of trouble just getting him to keep still.

"Is it okay if I go over to Donnie's after breakfast?" Gerald said, as he shoveled a forkful of pancakes into his mouth.

"You make sure you put on your winter coat and gloves," she told him.

He looked up from his plate, frowning. "But Mom, I only have to walk from here to Donnie's house—"

"You do as you're told: coat and gloves, mister. In case you hadn't noticed there's a blizzard coming. And you stay indoors, young man."

Gerald sighed. "Yes, Mom." He wiped his mouth and stood to take his plate to the sink and charged out of the kitchen, eager for the day's play, when he suddenly collided with his father.

"Whoa there, Gerry!" Lucas Forsyth said, taking his son gently by the shoulders. "There a fire or something in here?"

Gerald smiled and gripped his father about the waist, breathing in the smell of newsprint.

"Dad—you're home!"

Lucas smiled down at his son and Gerald mentally counted the number of ink smudges on his father's face.

"I hope you haven't been giving your mother a hard time?" Lucas said, offering his wife a wink.

"No, Dad, I was just about to get ready to go over to Donnie's so we can plan for the big day."

Lucas frowned. "What big day?"

"Halloween, Dad! You know: trick-or-treating. How could you forget?"

Lucas ruffled his boy's fine sandy hair. "I didn't forget, Gerry. I know that it's Halloween." He paused. "But I'm not sure we'll be able to go trick-or-treating this year."

Gerald's jaw dropped. "But we do it every year! Every year you take me and Donnie out trick-or-treating. Donnie says he has our costumes ready and everything!"

Lucas cupped Gerald's face in his huge hands. "I know that Gerry, but I just heard on the radio that there's a big snowstorm coming in. Biggest one in nearly fifty years, they're saying."

Bethany suddenly chimed in, her hands deep in dishwater. "There's no way you are going out in that blizzard, Gerald Forsyth. I don't care if it is Halloween."

"But Mom!" Gerald protested, but his father turned his face back so he could look him squarely in the eye.

"Hey, you listen now. Your mother's right, Gerry, it's not safe to go out there. Maybe the blizzard will blow right by us, but if it doesn't, well, it's not the end of the world if we miss Halloween. We can always go next year."

Gerald's bottom lip bulged. "But it's our family tradition, Dad. We go every year—you, me, Donnie and Donnie's dad."

Lucas crouched down to his son's level. "I know Gerry, I know. Let's just wait and see what happens with the storm, okay? Now, you go upstairs and your Mom and I will talk about whether you can go see Donnie, okay?"

"Okay, Dad." Gerald said. The boy walked mournfully out of the kitchen, his eyes on the floor all the way as he walked up the stairs to his bedroom. He got dressed slowly and sighed heavily, like life had suddenly become a chore. He looked through his bedroom window and cursed the snow, which was being "totally unfair" by ruining a perfectly good Halloween.

While Donnie waited, frost had begun to creep across the glass of Gerald's bedroom window. The street outside was coated in white, and the more Gerald watched the thicker the snow became, swirling and falling with determination. The prospect of simply going next door to visit his friend—let alone trick-or-treating—became more and more remote.

Gerald sighed, defeated. He turned back to look at his unmade bed, the desire to just fall into it and give up on his favorite holiday tugging at his mind. He was about to do just that when a loud thump suddenly resounded behind him. He whirled on his feet to see a large splodge of snow sliding down the window pane. The ridiculous notion that the snowflakes were getting bigger made him shake his head, but the abrupt squeal of white noise from his walkie talkie made him jump.

"Ger…ry!" a voice said.

He stepped to his dresser drawer to retrieve the walkie talkie and pressed the receiver.

"Donnie—is that you?"

"Co…m to…wind—!" the voice crackled.

Gerald turned the squelch dial down on his walkie talkie, but the crackling only became more incessant, the storm dominating everything.

"Say again, Donnie?"

"I said…to the…dow!"

Gerald stepped to the window and peered down through the gaps in the frost to the front lawn. He saw his friend standing ankle deep in the snow, wrapped in a heavy winter coat, scarf, mittens and woolen cap. Donnie seemed to fade in and out in the falling snow, like a light bulb on its last legs. Gerald slid open the window and the snow swarmed in his room.

"What are you doing?" Gerald cried through the wind.

Donnie cupped his gloved hands around his mouth. "You gotta come down here and play—it's awesome!"

"But…the blizzard?"

"Chicken!" Donnie fired back.

"Mom and Dad won't let me go outside. They say there's a really bad storm coming and we might not be able to go trick-or-treating tonight!"

"Yeah, that's what my Dad said, but what do they know, right? Come on, get your sled and we'll hit the snow!"

Gerald hesitated; he wanted to chase Donnie away, slam the window shut and accept defeat, but Donnie was already outside and the snowstorm didn't look so bad. In fact, the snow looked like it would be a hell of a lot of fun.

When Gerald was certain his mother was busy in the linen cupboard looking for more blankets, and his father was down for a nap, he snuck outside through the back door into a world of white.

He found Donnie sitting on the curb, his coat powdered with snow. Gerald pulled up the hood of his own coat, secured the earmuffs of his bomber hat and ran stealthily across the lawn to meet him. He noticed immediately that Donnie didn't have his own sled with him.

"Where's your sled?" Gerald said.

Donnie smiled and shook his head. "Don't worry about that—we're not going sledding."

"What?"

"We're going trick-or-treating."

Gerald's eyes widened. He opened his mouth to seek more of an explanation when Donnie promptly turned and ran across the street—Blake Street—towards an oak tree on the other side. Through the snowfall, Gerald could just make out Donnie rummaging inside a bag of some kind. Gerald, reminding himself that Donnie could be frustratingly unpredictable, had little choice but to trot after him. The freezing air burned inside his nostrils.

"Donnie, what's going on? We can't go trick-or-treating in this weather."

Donnie peered deep inside his bag. "You want to celebrate Halloween, don't you? You want candy, right?"

Gerald tried to rub more warmth into the arms of his coat and looked at the snow slowly erasing every detail of Blake Street.

"Yes, but I don't know, Donnie—I think it might be too cold. I think we should go back home."

Donnie stopped searching in his bag and lifted his face to shake his head condescendingly at his friend. His green eyes narrowed and curls of his hair waved in the wind.

"Have you forgotten our promise?"

Gerald sighed. "No."

"We said that we'd never miss a Halloween, no matter what. That's what we said."

"I know that, but this storm is crazy, Donnie."

Donnie pulled a bundle of clothing out of his bag and shoved it into Gerald's hands. "It's not that bad—now put this on!"

Gerald looked at the bundle in his hands and a sneering face stared back at him: a pale white face, with red lips and blood-streaked fangs. Gerald was looking at the rubbery depiction of the great Count Dracula. The mask swam within a large black polyester cape. Gerald had to stifle a look of glee.

"We're really going to do this?" he said. "Donnie, no one will open their front door in this cold."

"Just put it on!" Donnie told him as he retrieved his own mask and jacket ensemble from the bag.

Gerald watched as his friend pulled on a putrescent green face. Its forehead was elongated and bore garishly painted scars. Two silver-painted rubber bolts protruded from the neck. The unmistakable face of the Frankenstein monster, modelled after the great Boris Karloff. When Donnie gave the mask a downward pull Gerald recalled a painting he'd once seen in a school book of a person on a bridge screaming. To complete his costume, Donnie put on an over-sized navy blue suit jacket, covered in old mud and ropy gobs of red poster paint. Donnie struggled to get it over his winter coat, but the doubling up of clothes certainly gave him that muscled look. Gerald couldn't help but laugh.

"You look fat," Gerald teased.

"Do not!" Donnie said out of the corner of his mouth. He sniffed hard and rubbed his nose, then he pulled a small tube of green poster paint from the suit pocket, squeezed it into his palm and rubbed it all over the mask and his neck for good measure.

"Aww gross!" Gerald said, grimacing at how authentically undead his friend now appeared.

"Didn't you see the movie poster for Frankenstein? He's green—so I have to be green too. There's some of my mom's make up in the bag and some fake blood. Put some on your face and let's go."

Gerald shook his head. "Donnie I really think we should just go home."

His friend wiped his paint-smeared hands on his jacket and Gerald, assuming the jacket was Donnie's father's, didn't think that was a good idea.

"We do this every year—we can't stop now. If we start door knocking now, we should get most of the street done before the storm gets any worse. So, are you coming or not?"

Gerald looked down at his mask and cape; he'd been so excited about Halloween and he couldn't believe a blizzard was going to ruin it. He watched Donnie zip up his bag; it looked as if he was going trick-or-treating—with or without his friend.

"Donnie, we really shouldn't—" he began.

"Oh, shouldn't what?" Donnie said, his impatience making his Frankenstein face look even more menacing.

"Nothing." Gerald slipped the cape over his shoulders and it billowed in the wind. He pulled on the mask and through the narrow eye slits he saw Donnie smiling wildly.

"Awesome! You look so cool, Gerry! Come on—let's go!"

Dracula and Frankenstein ran away from the tree then towards number three Blake Street, leaving a trail of ghostly snowflakes in their wake.

Mrs. Doris Farley barely opened her door a crack when Donnie and Gerald knocked on it. She gawked at them in disbelief over her half-moon glasses.

"What in the name of all that's good and holy are you boys doing outside? Don't you know there's a storm coming?"

Donnie held out his bag and bared his teeth, trying to look as a monster should.

"It's Halloween, Mrs. Farley," he said.

"You boys need to get on back home. It's too cold to be trick-or-treating."

"Please, Mrs. Farley," Donnie whined. "We just want to get some candy. Do you have any?"

A gust of wind burst onto Mrs. Farley's porch, sending a swarm of snowflakes right into her face. Her subsequent squeal would have given a banshee a run for its money. She slammed the door, but not before she said: "Go home, before you freeze to death!"

The pair were left standing on the porch, shoulder to shoulder for warmth; Dracula and Frankenstein, the reanimated dead.

"What are we going to do now, Donnie?" Gerald said. "No one is going to answer their door to give us candy!"

Donnie turned and walked down the stairs, scanning Blake Street. Gerald wondered what he was looking at because all he could see was white; the storm hung over Duluth like a death shroud.

"We can't just give up after one house," Donnie told him. "What about Mr. Colton's over on Washington Street? Mrs. Colton's always nice—she gave us home-made peanut brittle last year—remember?"

Gerald nodded at the recollection of how good Mrs. Colton's peanut brittle was. "Maybe she'll invite us in for a cup of cocoa?"

"Yeah," Donnie said before sniffing and rubbing his nose again.

Gerald pushed his friend's shoulder playfully. "Have you been picking your nose again? It'll make it bleed, doofus!"

"Shut up—at least it'd make my costume look more real."

The two of them laughed in agreement and broke into a sprint towards Washington Street. They playfully jostled for front position, laughing, forgetting about the blizzard and remembering that Halloween was all about having fun.

Gerald laughed as they ran through the snow towards the intersection of Blake and Washington. Behind him, he could hear Donnie giving chase, his boots crunching the snow, which must have been at least two feet thick on the ground now.

"Last one's a rotten egg!" Gerald teased over his shoulder at Donnie. "Or is that…a rotten corpse!"

Gerald saw Washington Street before him: the houses nestled together, inviting yellow light glowing from the windows. But it was just as Gerald came to the point where Washington merged with Blake Street that he suddenly felt…strange. He came to a stop and stared at his boots. A moment later Donnie appeared at his side, puffing and panting.

"What's the matter?" he asked.

Gerald looked at the road surface beneath his feet, squeezed his eyes shut and then re-opened them.

"The road," he said.

Donnie looked at the road. "Yeah, it's a road—so what?"

Gerald pointed at it as if his friend couldn't see it for looking. "There's no snow on it."

Gerald watched as the realization slowly emerged on his

friend's face; a slight dip in his eyebrows, a quizzical upwards curve at the corner of his mouth.

"What—how?" Donnie said.

Gerald held out his gloved hands to the air; not a single snowflake fell on the intersection. Curiosity getting the better of him, he turned on his heels a full 180 degrees to look behind him, back up Blake Street. His gloves slowly filled up with snowflakes. Donnie copied Gerald and gasped.

"Man, that is so cool!" he said.

"It's weird," Gerald replied, turning back to stand in the center of the intersection. "Don't you think it's weird that the snow isn't falling here on this spot?

Donnie sniffed and rubbed his nose. "Yeah, it's a little weird, but who cares—come on, let's go to the Colton's already."

"I don't know, Donnie." Gerald couldn't take his eyes off the unblemished, grey asphalt.

Donnie shoved his friend with one hand, while he rubbed his nose again with the other. "Don't be such a baby. It's probably just the wind or something blowing up the street." He took a step onto Washington. "Dammit!"

"What—what's wrong?" Gerald asked, suddenly afraid to move.

Donnie stared down at his own gloved hands. "My nose!"

Gerald saw the droplets of blood on Donnie's gloves, watched them soak into the wool. He drew his eyes up and saw a steady drip of blood falling from his friend's left nostril, almost like a running tap.

"Oh, no!" Gerald said, stepping off the curb onto the road towards Donnie.

The blood dripped onto the sleeve of Donnie's jacket, down and down to spatter across his boots. Donnie quickly clamped his hands over his nose and squeezed to stem the flow. His brown gloves became red.

"It won't stop!" Donnie cried through his hands. His eyes were wide with panic.

Gerald knew Donnie occasionally had nosebleeds, but never one this bad. "Move your hand!" he told Donnie, reaching up to pry his hands away. "Let me have a look!"

Donnie complied, dropping his hands. The blood was running down over his lips.

"Aw gross!" Donnie said, before turning to spit a great job of blood onto the road. It hit the asphalt with an audible slap.

Abruptly the wind stopped howling. There was only the road, yet it was more dirt than asphalt. All the houses had disappeared; there was only the crossroads, and the two boys. Gerald and Donnie looked around them. The sky was blue and cloudless. The air was warm, so warm they felt the urge to take off their winter coats.

"Where are we?" Gerald said.

Donnie let go of his nose and realized it had stopped bleeding.

"What's happening?" he said to Gerald.

The landscape was lush and green, apart from the dirt crossroads beneath their feet. There were no structures of any kind, only a large oak tree, which cast a looming shadow over the pair. Gerald's heart hammered against his ribs.

"Donnie—I don't understand…"

The sound of a branch snapping made them turn. The oak tree was thick, its bark rippled and veined with age. The leaves were turning gold, heralding the rapid approach of Fall.

"What was that?" Donnie said.

"I…don't know."

There was more rustling, too loud to simply be the wind. Then again, there was no wind, only the harshness of the sun and the tree's shadow.

"Hello? Who's there?" Gerald said in the direction of the tree.

The rustling ceased at the sound of Gerald's direct question and a shape emerged from behind the tree's broad trunk: a person. The boys saw the silhouette and wanted to run, but something even more powerful than their fear fixed them to the spot.

The stooped, thin figure shuffled towards them, bleeding out of the tree's grey shadow to reveal itself as a woman. Her hair was knotted and black, her skirts torn, corset coming apart at the seams. These aspects, however, paled in comparison to her face, which was the color of ancient death.

There was no mistaking she was dead; the way her head rested on an angle, the way the bones of her neck bulged beneath her parchment skin. Her neck had clearly been broken—and viciously. In her gnarled right hand she held the noose that had performed the deed.

"Hello, little ones," the woman said, her voice echoing behind them, beside them and above them.

The boys instinctively came closer to each other, out of fear.

"Is she…dead?" Donnie said, keeping his voice low.

"I…don't know," Gerald said.

"But look at her neck."

The woman's grey eyes moved from Donnie to Gerald and back again, yet her eyelids never blinked; she simply stared at them from that awful askew angle. She stepped towards them, her left foot dragging in the dirt. The boys took a step backwards in response.

"It's been an age since anyone has visited me," the woman said through leathery lips. "So very long."

"We'd like to go home now, please," Gerald said, very slowly, carefully.

The woman turned her head to look at Gerald and her skull lolled forward, grinding shattered vertebrae together.

"Already?" The lips curled downward. "You have only just arrived; please stay and talk with me."

"How did we get here?" Donnie asked, glancing furtively at the tree.

She reached up with her right hand and, very precisely, touched the tip of her crooked nose.

"Your blood, child—your blood summoned me to you."

Donnie stared at the dried blood on his gloves and suddenly felt disgust. He tore the gloves from his hands and threw them on the ground.

"I don't want to be here anymore!" he said to the woman. "I want to go home!"

Gerald looked at Donnie's gloves on the ground, in the dirt; the great dusty crossroad which seemed to stretch off into the horizon for all eternity. He suddenly understood.

"We're still on Washington Avenue!" he said, half-smiling at his epiphany. When he looked up from the road he saw Donnie and the woman scrutinizing him curiously.

"Such a clever child," the woman said.

Donnie turned to his friend. "But how? This doesn't look anything like home. It's not even snowing here!"

The woman shuffled closer, her lips cracking with a smile, revealing jaundiced teeth nestled between oil-black gums.

"You are still there, yet you are also here at the same time—and in between."

"What does that mean?" Donnie shouted, his whole body shaking with confused rage. Gerald reached out and gripped his arm in a bid to calm him.

"It's okay, Donnie—we'll figure this out and get back home, all right?"

Donnie swallowed and fought back the tears welling in his terrified green eyes. Gerald offered him a reassuring smile, but inside he wanted to scream. Once he knew his friend had calmed down he turned to address the woman.

"What do you want…with us?"

Her eyes narrowed. "I want freedom."

"Freedom?"

"I have been imprisoned here for a very long time and I want to leave."

Gerald thought he saw sadness in her eyes, but how could someone who was clearly dead feel sorrow?

"So, you want us to help you?"

"Yes."

"Then how?" Donnie chimed in, impatient.

She turned, or rather staggered, to the center of the crossroads. "This has been my cage for three centuries—ever since they hanged me as a witch."

"A witch?" Gerald said.

"They claimed I cavorted with devils; let him put his cold prick inside me. They even said I gave birth to his spawn. My neighbors dragged me here to this tree and hanged me like a chandelier for all to see!"

Gerald swallowed hard, easily imagining the noose in her hand being coiled around her neck, the bones snapping.

"Ever since that day," the woman continued, "I have been waiting for someone to come—to take my place. I believed that eventually some poor soul in the land of the living would lose their lives on this spot—be it by accident, or more sinister means—but I never dreamed a few drops of virgin blood could bring me my salvation."

She stepped to them again, her arms reaching, gnarled fingers bending like spider's legs.

"One of you must take my place!" she hissed.

"No!" Donnie cried, recoiling from her approach.

Strangely, and suddenly, neither boy could move. The woman circled them and despite the midday sun beating down on the landscape, a foul chill emanated from her body. The skin of Gerald and Donnie's arms bristled with goose pimples beneath their coats.

"Oh, and yet you will choose, my young pups—or both of you will die!"

"How can we choose?" Donnie said, sobbing, his body rigid through magic—or fear.

She moved behind them and placed her dry, icy fingers on the backs of their heads, like a mother ruffling her child's hair.

"Perhaps it will not be such a challenge for two friends who trust each other?" she said, before circling again to face them. "You came here through blood—it is only fitting that blood should be part of the trial." She traced both of their faces with a clawed finger. "You are close friends, yes?"

"Yes," they replied, and their voices wavered with terror.

"Perhaps even as close as…brothers?" she asked further.

Donnie and Gerald turned their eyes to each other, then answered *yes* once more. The woman clapped her hands and revealed a slimy grin.

"Splendid! Now, have you heard of the term 'sworn blood brothers'?"

"No," Gerald said, but Donnie interjected:

"Yes—I know it!" he said. "My father told me about it once.

He said it's like a...a promise you make. A 'blood oath', I think he called it. He even showed me. He took a knife and cut his palm and then he cut me and we shook hands."

"That's it!" The woman smiled wider and a string of drool slid from her lips.

Gerald didn't like the concept of the "blood oath"; the mingling of blood. Seeing Donnie's nose bleeding was bad enough, so what exactly was this woman proposing?

She leaned into them and took their hands and it was like they'd both been forced inside a meat locker.

"Please let us go," Donnie said, but the woman pressed a finger to his lips.

"Hush now, child. It's too late for that; begging won't help you. You must listen to Martha now. One of you must stay here so I can leave, but I cannot make that choice—it has to be decided between the two of you."

Gerald felt tear on his cheeks, tasted snot on his lips. He wanted to scream for his mother, but she was impossibly far away. Martha smiled at him before turning her gaze to his friend.

"You boy—what be your name?"

"Donnie, ma'am," he said quickly.

"Donnie, I want to thank you—for opening the door and finding me. Your blood was the key that unlocked me from my cage of woe. A pity, I need you to shed much more."

"What?" Donnie's eyes widened.

Martha waited, savoring the boys' reactions. Gerald knew she was asking them to perform some sort of ritual; asking them to hurt themselves—or each other.

"I'm not going to hurt Gerry," Donnie said, and Gerald could tell he was putting to put a lot of bravery into his voice.

"Then you will die here right now," Martha replied.

Donnie shook his head, a pendulum run on fear. "I can't—please don't make me!"

Gerald felt his pulse in his throat. A wave of nausea clenched around his stomach and he struggled to fight the urge not to vomit.

"This is not a request," Martha told Donnie. Donnie was sobbing now, spittle bubbling between his downturned lips.

"No—I won't hurt him!"

"I demand blood!" Martha howled, and the entire landscape seemed to flicker under the power of her voice, like a light bulb at death's door.

Gerald watched as Martha moved behind Donnie. She placed her hands on his shoulders and eyed Gerald coyly. Miraculously, Donnie could once more move his body, but Martha still gripped him tight. She leaned down to speak into Donnie's ear, all the while never taking her eyes off Gerald.

"Kill your friend," she said, and Gerald heard her every word.

Donnie's arms rose up from his side. He looked so much like Frankenstein, a shambling horror reaching out for the nearest throat, and Gerald feared it would be his if he didn't act. He saw Donnie's face, his eyeballs so white, his lips mouthing at Gerald to "run", his nose dripping mucous-stringed blood.

Blood.

Self-preservation overtook Gerald's will and somehow, he managed to slip Martha's psychic grasp. He lunged at Donnie and punched him as hard as he could in the face. Donnie toppled backwards, falling to the ground. Gerald straddled him, raining down a barrage of blows until Donnie's face burst with fresh blood.

Between the pounding blows and the cascading waves of agony through his little fingers, Gerald thought of home. Of his mother and father, worried sick about where he was, of the freezing white snow falling upon Blake Street. If he was to escape and survive this nightmare, then Donnie Psalter would have to die. So, he wrapped his now slick red hands around Frankenstein's throat and squeezed.

*He's not Donnie—he's Frankenstein—and Frankenstein is a monster, so he has to die.*

And only Dracula could kill him.

When Frankenstein's eyes finally rolled back in his skull, the whites glinting in the perpetual noonday sun, Gerald released his grip. He stood and looked down at Frankenstein's body for many moments, in awe of how still the monster was.

"He's dead," Gerald said to himself.

"Yes," Martha said, almost sighing with pleasure. She went to Gerald and embraced him, cold thin arm bones creaking loudly. "I always knew it would be you," she said. Then she smiled at him and faded into the air like a dust mote.

The sunlit vista evaporated with her, plunging Gerald back into his wintry world, back to Blake Street. He found himself standing on the same crossroad, but without Frankenstein. Frankenstein had been left behind—to take Martha's place for all eternity.

Eventually, the snow began to fall onto the intersection; the barrier that held it at bay removed. Gerald watched the snowflakes drift around him and after a long while, his mind felt clearer, calmer. He took off his Dracula cape and mask and stepped off the intersection onto Blake Street—towards home.

He found his parents standing at the front door, talking to Donnie's parents and a pair of police officers. They were frantic, accosting him with tear-streaked eyes and never-ending questions. They all wanted to know where he'd been, but it wasn't until they asked about Donnie that Gerald truly realized what he'd done.

As he sobbed over and over into his mother's arms, Gerald told them that his friend was gone, but he didn't know why or where.

That knowledge would only ever come to him when he slept, in the form of nightmares.

## 7

No matter how many times Kelli wiped the tears away, they kept on coming.

She stared at Gerald through those same tears, as if she were looking at the world through his sorrow; as if she'd become infected by it.

"I…I just don't believe it," she said.

The old man frowned. "It's true," he said, and he was adamant.

"No—no, I mean I believe you—it's hard not to when the evidence is right outside that door. It's just that the story sounds so…impossible."

Gerald rubbed his hands together, feeling their roughness,

their age. "I've lived with that story all my life. He sighed and sagged in his chair. "You're the first person I've told the truth."

"What—you never even told your parents—or Donnie's parents?"

"What could I tell them—that Donnie exchanged his soul so a witch could go free?"

Kelli cringed, her sympathy waning once more. "So, you just lied?"

"I had to!"

"You *had to?*" Kelli couldn't believe his arrogance. "He was your friend!"

"Donnie was dead! Don't you understand? He was gone; lost to that god-awful place. Telling the truth was never going to bring him back."

Kelli turned her eyes to the door. "Yet, here he is."

Gerald looked at the door then and she could see that her words cut him deep, his eyes lost in despondency.

"He's here to torment me—to make me suffer, just as he does. He comes to visit me every anniversary—every Halloween. All I can do is lock the door and wait for him to go away."

"I don't blame him for wanting you to suffer," Kelli said.

Now Gerald was the one to look appalled. "I beg your pardon?"

"I only feel sorry for Donnie," she told him. "Maybe if you'd told the truth—maybe if you hadn't killed him in the first place then none of this would even be happening!"

Gerald almost rose from his wheelchair. "You think I don't know that?! Don't you think I haven't thought about that every day since he was taken? It wasn't my fault—it was hers! That witch! She gave me no choice!"

Kelli almost spat: "There's always a choice!"

"Really—then what would you have done? Tell me Miss High-and-Mighty, what would you have done?!"

She avoided his furious eyes. "I…I don't know. But I wouldn't have left my friend there to rot."

Gerald pointed an arthritic finger at her. "Don't you judge me—you have no idea of the sacrifices I had to make. I had to tell his family that he was abducted, for God's sake! I sat in the back of a police car for hours—days—while they looked for Donnie, all the while knowing that everything I'd told them was a lie. In the years after that day my childhood was hell. My parents took me to counselling every week until I was thirteen. I became a laughing stock at school. I even flunked out of college, forced to come back here and live with my parents. I think they must have been happy when they died, knowing they didn't have to burden themselves with me any longer."

Kelli stood and touched the door; she knew every inch of its flecked paint, every grain of wood beneath, but only because of what stood on the other side of it.

"You talk about suffering and sacrifices, but what about the sacrifice Donnie made—hmm? He's dead—and you're still here."

The old man lifted himself up out of his chair, arms trembling with weakness, his face crimson with rage.

"I wish I was dead!"

The timbre of his voice almost knocked Kelli off her feet and it left Gerald hollow, his frame dropping like a stone back into the chair.

"I wish I'd been the one to die that day!" Gerald admitted. "Not Donnie. But I was just a boy—a little boy scared of never seeing his mother or father again. I wanted to live and I'm sorry—I'm so sorry that I have to say this, but it was either him…or me."

Kelli's lips curled in disgust. "And so, you chose you?"

"Yes—and I've regretted that choice ever since. I'll only ever be free of Donnie when I die—I know that."

Kelli remained quiet, overwhelmed by the silence, her distaste for Gerald's every word. She wondered if Donnie's ghost could hear them, hear Gerald's self-pity.

"Why don't you just tell him you're sorry?" she said.

"Oh, I've tried that! I've told him I was sorry a thousand times. I went to his grave so many times. I told my parents and his parents I was sorry so many times, but it was never enough. It tore both families apart and I'm certain it sent my mother and father to an early grave. I've apologized to Donnie every Halloween, but he still comes!"

"Did you mean it?"

"Screw you!"

"Oh, that's nice, Gerald! You know something—you're so-called suffering has left you an empty man, cold-hearted and weak. But out there is a boy who can never grow old, can never know love or see his family again because of you. And he'll certainly never rest in peace unless you let him!"

Gerald threw his hands in the air. "Then what would you have me do?!"

Kelli crouched down beside him and looked him in the face. She had to choose her words carefully if she was going to convince him to do the right thing.

"You have to accept what you did was wrong. You have to ask his forgiveness."

Gerald's brow wavered with self-doubt. "I can't."

"Put yourself in his shoes—you said yourself that could quite easily be you standing outside that door. Would you expect Donnie to say he was sorry?"

Gerald put his head in his hands and released a prolonged cry of grief, a cry that had been pent up for more than fifty years. Kelli thought the old man had snapped, the weight of anguish finally shattering his will. Her heart quickened when his keening suddenly became gasps for air.

"Are you alright?" Kelli said.

Gerald lifted his head to reveal eyes wide with fear, a mouth wide in desperation, beckoning breath.

"Can't—"

Kelli rummaged in the back of his wheelchair for the oxygen mask and put it over his face. She turned the dial on the oxygen canister, but there was no hiss of air being released. She sensed the oxygen was all gone and the only other canisters could be found outside in her car.

"Oh, God!" she cried. "Gerald—listen to me. You have to try and take some deep breaths, okay? In through your nose and out through your mouth."

The old man clawed at the mask, as if it was useless. "Help—me!" he wheezed.

Kelli leant down behind the chair again and turned up the

dial to full. Still nothing came. She gazed up at him, her face a mask of defeat. Her expression melted to shock when she saw Gerald—straight-faced and breathing freely—raise his arm towards her face. He brought his elbow down hard across her face, plunging her into the black pool of unconsciousness.

Gerald checked Kelli's pulse and breathing, all the while telling her repeatedly how sorry he was. When he was certain she was fine, he took a towel from the rack near the shower, rolled it up and placed it beneath her head.

Grunting, he pulled himself back up into the wheelchair and wheeled around to face the door. It must have been the early hours of the morning now and the razor-sharp cold was starting to creep into his home. He should have been in bed, but he'd stopped sleeping on Halloween a long time ago and now that his past had finally found a way into his home, he couldn't afford not to keep his eyes open.

He reached for the door handle, only to hesitate. He glanced back over his shoulder to look down at Kelli lying in a state of unawareness on the floor. He liked Kelli; she meant well, but she was wrong to think that Donnie was ever going to forgive him for what he did. There was only one thing Donnie's ghost would ever accept.

An exchange of souls.

The bathroom door creaked open onto a shadow-soaked hallway. As quickly as he could, Gerald wheeled himself out of the bathroom and closed the door behind him, sealing Kelli safely inside.

Gerald scanned the sleeping world of his home, his old eyes struggling to adjust to the absence of light. He wheeled up the hallway towards the kitchen, often checking over his shoulder for the unmistakable silhouette of his eternal tormentor.

The wheelchair suddenly jerked forward, gathering pace. Gerald turned in his seat and saw the specter of his childhood friend had control of his chair and was wheeling him through the house up the hall and back to the living room.

"Donnie—stop!" Gerald cried as the hallway rushed past him.

The wheelchair barreled onwards, knocking into a display cabinet. The momentum caused the chair to tilt and Gerald tumbled out, landing hard on the living room floor. The old man rolled onto his back to look up at Donnie. The ghost child tossed the wheelchair aside and staggered towards Gerald, his cold, grey hands outstretched in search in vengeance.

"Don't!" Gerald screamed. "Wait!"

Donnie stopped and slowly lowered his hands to his sides, his lurid, Frankenstein head cocked to one side in curiosity. Gerald was amazed the boy seemed to understand him; seemed interested in having a conversation.

So, what to say to a friend you damned to hell?

"Donnie I…" Gerald began, and the ghost looked eager to hear more, taking a step closer. "I know I've said sorry to you many times before…and I know that's not what you want to hear."

Donnie straightened and his eyes were like hooks, reeling Gerald in. The old man swallowed before continuing.

"So…I'll say what you do want to hear." He took a deep breath and his chest retaliated with a wheeze. "I deserve to die. I deserve whatever it is you want to dish out to me. I know that. I should be punished for what I did and all these years I've just been delaying the inevitable. I think…deep down…that I did really die that day, but it just took my body a hell of a long time to catch up. And I'm still a coward in the face of death.

"So if you want to kill me and drag my miserable excuse for a soul away with you, then be my guest. I'm not gonna stop you."

Donnie's ghost remained silent, but not still. Gerald watched as he turned and walked to the front door, reaching out with a frosted hand to unlock it. Then he turned back to face the old man, still with that same blank expression.

"You want me to go outside with you?" Gerald said.

Donnie's eyes spoke for him, pools of beckoning. Gerald nodded in acknowledgement and rose up to his knees, his weary bones protesting; his lungs sacks of broken glass.

"Okay," he said. "Just give me a sec." He pulled himself to his feet and felt a wave of dizziness. He thought he would fall again, almost as if his body was getting ready to finally give up his ghost. He shuffled to the front door, eventually coming to a halt at Donnie's side. His end was in sight.

He looked down at Donnie. The boy's nose had stopped bleeding some time ago and there was a thin layer of glittering frost coating his body. The boy's time in the cold and the dark was hopefully about to end too.

"I'm ready, Donnie," he said.

Donnie reached out and turned the doorknob to open the door. Blake Street was bathed in a dull purple fog. To the east, Gerald could see the first blood red sliver of the new dawn. Halloween was drawing its curtains for another year. Donnie took Gerald's hand and walked him down the front steps to stand on the front lawn. Blake Street was quiet, all the trick-or-treaters curled up tight in their beds, deep in the grip of sugar-induced dreams of fancy.

Sleep: Gerald so wanted to sleep.

When he turned his head to say something to Donnie, the boy had somehow gone back inside and retrieved his wheelchair. The old man gratefully took his seat, wondering why Donnie was suddenly treating him with kindness.

As soon as he sat, there was a flash and when it faded a moment later Gerald discovered they were travelling along the sidewalk, Donnie wheeling him away from his house; in the direction of Blake and Washington.

"Oh," Gerald said, simultaneously fascinated and anxious. "We're going back here then? It's been a long time."

In the pre-dawn blackness, the only sound to be heard was the creaking of the wheels on the sidewalk, the tremor of his heart and the wheeze in his chest. The very air seemed to crackle with energy as they approached the intersection. Donnie brought their procession to a halt in the middle of the street and the boy walked around to face his long-lost friend.

"What do you want me to do now?" Gerald asked him.

Donnie's mute ghost waited patiently.

"What—what are we supposed to do?" Gerald said.

His chest rattled and Gerald felt a blockage in his chest. He began to cough harshly, the effort becoming involuntary and incessant. He covered his mouth with his hand as a great gob of blood burst from his lips into his palm. He gaped at the stark redness of it as it dribbled between his fingers, down to the asphalt beneath their feet.

Light struck them then as the world split in two. Through the veil of reality, Gerald could see the wide green mirage he'd first witnessed with his friend so many years before. When he looked at Donnie, the boy appeared brand new; clean and fresh, almost alive. Yet there was no life in his face.

Gerald smiled in wonder at the sight of him, at the world on the other side. If his punishment meant he had to spend eternity with his friend here, then maybe that wouldn't be so bad.

"You know the real reason I've hated Halloween for all these years, Donnie?" Gerald said. The boy turned to look at him forlornly and shook his head.

Gerald said: "Because I never got to spend all those Halloweens with you."

Gerald smiled anew and they were moving again, Donnie silently wheeling him through the crack to the other side. In the distance, Gerald saw the great oak tree, its top leaves glistening emeralds in the ever-midday sun. Beneath the tree was shadow, a lush cool place to spend the rest of—

Gerald saw one of the shadows beneath the tree move: a thin, wiry silhouette, gangly and broken, hair swaying as she walked. Gerald gasped as realization gripped his chest, but his lungs failed him and as his soul left his body Martha smiled and claimed it for her own.

Kelli could see herself from the outside in. She was lying on the bathroom floor, cold in unconsciousness. Her point of view swelled, rose so she could take in the entire room from above. She saw herself on the floor and Gerald Forsyth curled up in the corner, riddled with guilt.

The bathroom door crashed open in a swarm of splinters

and white mist. The shape of Donnie slinked into the room, his silhouette like a knife. His grubby, frozen fingers reached out for Gerald, clasping around the old man's throat. In seconds Gerald froze over, encased in a tomb of ice, sheer terror forever etched in his face.

As the boy turned his attention to Kelli's unconscious form, she came to, as if roused from a nightmare. Her scream was muffled as Donnie plunged his burning cold fingers into her mouth, filling her up with icy death from the inside out.

Kelli woke on the bathroom floor, screaming. Her heart trampolined in her chest and only slowed when the miasma of shock cleared. Realizing it was only a dream she sucked in deep, calming breaths and scanned the room.

The last thing she remembered was Gerald striking her in the head. Oh, boy, would she give him a piece of her mind when she found him.

It was at that moment she realized Gerald Forsyth wasn't in the room—and the door was wide open.

*Oh, God!*

Kelli scrambled to her feet and stepped out into the hallway. Furtively, she looked over the house from where she stood. Dawn was slowly painting the world in vermillion. She could barely think for the sound of her terrified heart.

She saw no sign Gerald—or the boy. Had Donnie finally gotten hold of the old man? She sincerely hoped not. She so wanted a happy ending to this nightmare; anything but Gerald's death. She did like him, despite his faults; he was still a fellow human being, who didn't deserve to die at the hands of some supernatural evil.

Slowly, she walked up the hallway to the living room. The house was empty and a frosty breeze from the open front door told Kelli the boy and the old man must have gone outside. Kelli ran out onto the porch, desperately hoping she'd find them standing on the front lawn, but to no avail.

Seeing the street was devoid of anyone, Kelli instinctively ran to the next house and banged on the front door. After a few moments a man in his mid-40s, unshaven and half-awake answered the door with a look that could have even rivalled Donnie Psalter's.

"Call the police!" Kelli told him.

"Say what?"

"Call the police—your neighbor, Gerald Forsyth, has been abducted!"

Kelli's final word seemed to get the man's attention and instantly he went back into his house to pick up the phone. Kelli left him to his task and ran into the street, past so many sleeping houses, everyone completely oblivious to what had happened on Halloween night—what was still happening. She felt like she should knock on every door and warn them, but her only priority was Gerald—her patient.

As she approached the intersection of Blake and Washington, she glimpsed a figure standing in the middle of the street.

"Gerald!" Kelli cried.

The figure turned towards her voice. It wasn't Gerald, but rather a woman, tall, slender, to the point of being anorexic. She wore a nightgown, fastened with a thin cord, of all things. Yet it was her face that made Kelli flinch; like thin leather stretched over a bulbous skull. Her eyes were the color of oil and her hair like snakes. The woman's head was awkwardly cocked to one side.

"Alas, poor Gerald's gone now," the woman said.

"I'm sorry?" Kelli replied.

The strange woman smiled, revealing yellow teeth. "He's with me now," she said. "Through the veil; you shan't be seeing him again."

"What are you talking about?" Kelli tried to mentally get her heart to slow down, but something about this woman kept her fear center firing.

"I had Donnie collect him—they deserve to be together, those two."

"How do you know about Donnie—" Kelli stopped mid-sentence and clamped a hand over her mouth. This made the woman smile even wider.

"Gerald Forsyth's childhood tale was mostly true," Martha said. "All except the part where I told him and Donnie that I weren't a witch."

"Oh, my God!" Kelli said, sobbing.

The witch took a step backward and the space behind her split like a torn seam. Through the gap in reality Kelli made out a wide expanse of hills, but they were grey, not green; dead and gone. And a fierce storm was brewing.

"No one ever escapes from my crossroads," Martha said. "They all come home to me eventually—you'd do well to remember that."

With those final words, she was gone, swallowed into hell; her, Donald Psalter and Gerald Forsyth with her—forever.

It wasn't until she felt a hand on her shoulder that Kelli remembered to breathe. She turned and found Gerald's neighbor with his wife and children, gawking at her.

"Miss—did you find him? Did you find Gerald?" the man said.

Kelli stared at the children—two little boys. After a moment she shook her head.

"No," she said. "He's gone."

Kelli looked from the boys to their parents. "You keep those boys away from that corner—you hear me? You keep all the children away!"

The man frowned. "Excuse me?"

Kelli ignored him, running past them to the police car that was turning into Blake Street. She had to find a way to warn them about the corner of Blake and Washington; about the witch that lived there. But most of all she had to warn them about Halloween.

# HAPPY DAZE

Harvey Dutton sat in front of the bathroom mirror and put on his true face.

First, he applied a thick white greasepaint with his fingers, spreading it evenly. Black stubble poked through the white, but he doubted the kids would mind or even notice. Next, he applied blue mascara around his left eye and green around the right. Harvey always enjoyed the feel of the brush on his eyelids, smooth and soft. Then, he reached for his red lipstick pen.

He drew a large, exaggerated smile on his lips, circling his entire mouth and stretching the line up his cheeks. He smiled to make sure the shape was just so. Then, finally, he put on his fuzzy rainbow wig. The sight of it and his great big red smile filled him with a deep warmth because he was no longer Harvey Dutton.

He was Giggles the Clown.

Once his face was touch dry, Harvey undressed down to his Y-fronts and took his Giggles costume off the hook on the back of the bathroom door. The suit was a custom-made three-piece, which cost him $750 way back when. It was patterned with rainbow pinstripes and embellished with oversized gold buttons.

Harvey slipped the trousers out of the laundromat bag and pulled them on, careful to ensure the pinstripes lined up perfectly down the length of his legs. The kids would notice if they weren't. He was about to put on his shirt when three soft knocks resounded from the other side of the door.

"Harvey?"

It was his wife, Louisa. Harvey replaced his shirt on its hanger and opened the door. She seemed to recoil when she beheld him partially dressed in his clown costume, which Harvey found odd.

"Hey, hon," Harvey said. "I'm just getting ready. You can have the shower soon."

Louisa looked to the floor, and then back to him, but wouldn't look him in the eye.

"Everything okay?" Harvey asked.

Her throat bobbed up and down. "I-I need to talk to you," she said.

Harvey smirked, his big red mouth lifting at one corner. "Oh, sure. What is it?"

Louisa scratched the back of her sandy blonde head. "I meant to talk to you last night."

Harvey sensed something troubled his wife. He reached for her, but she took a step back. "Hey, what's wrong?" His red lips drooped.

She shook her head. "I-I can't do this."

"It's okay. We can talk later if you—"

Her headshake became more vigorous. "No, no. I mean this." She waved her hands at him.

Harvey shifted from one foot to the other. "What do you mean?"

She met his gaze. "How much longer are you going to keep doing this?"

His red mouth hung open like he was a dead fish. "Sorry?"

"You've been doing this for almost ten years, Harvey."

"Yeah..."

She folded her arms. Harvey had never seen his wife act so defensive before.

"Before we married, five years ago, you told me this clown act wasn't forever," Louisa said. "That you'd find a more serious job. Try and get back into theater."

He moved towards her again, but now she grimaced, lip peeled back in a sneer. "Lou, where is this coming from? You've never said anything about this before."

She ran a hand through her hair. "I've put up with this for a long time. Too long."

"Put up with?" Harvey's painted smile contradicted his confusion. "Lou, this is my job. My business. I was doing this when we met. You know how much it means to me."

"But it's not paying the bills, is it, Harvey? I've… We've been struggling for years to pay off this house. When's the last time we went out to a restaurant?"

The way she said his name, practically spitting it out. There was resentment there. Tears threatened to ruin Harvey's makeup, but he told himself he wouldn't cry.

"I-I know things have been hard, but the boys and I… We have something special with Happy Daze. It's a hell of a lot more rewarding than the theater. We make enough to get by. Besides, I don't do it for the money, Lou, I do it for those little kids. The ones in the cancer wards who need some joy in their lives."

Louisa pointed at her chest. "I need some joy in my life, too, Harvey. You get up every morning and put on this…this façade, and you don't even consider how that might make me feel. Well, I'll tell you. It makes me embarrassed."

Trickles of sweat ran down Harvey's bare back. "You're… you're ashamed of me?"

Louisa didn't say, but her eyes said it all. Until she *did* voice it: "Do you know what it's like for me to tell people what you do for a living?"

Harvey's red smile trembled. "So, what? I should just give it all up, then? Become a mechanic or something? Do you really want me to give up what makes me happy?"

She walked away from him, her voice trailing behind her. "You do whatever you want, Harvey. I don't care anymore."

The other clowns glared at Harvey as he walked through the doors of *Happy Daze: Clowns for Hire.*

Pogo, Squeaks, and Zany all regarded him with indifference instead of their usual broad red smiles, and he wondered why he'd bothered to go to work at all.

Louisa's revelations left him feeling like he'd been torn right down the middle, like she'd reached into his chest, plucked out his heart, and flushed it down the toilet. Now, as he looked into the faces of his fellow clowns—his only friends—he had a bad feeling they wouldn't care, even if he told them.

"Where the hell have you been?" Pogo said, his white jowls trembling beneath his big red clown nose.

Harvey put his lunch inside his locker. "Sorry, guys. There's… there's been some trouble at home."

Pogo jabbed a chubby finger in his direction. He was shirtless, his stomach barely contained by his sequined suspenders. "Well, I had to cover your hour at the cancer ward, which meant I missed the birthday party already booked across town. The parents were livid and demanded a refund. Which means we're five hundred bucks short."

Harvey sighed. "Oh, man, I'm sorry, Red. I just…" A lump formed in his throat. "Louisa told me she's leaving me."

Pogo turned to Squeaks and Zany, and Harvey noticed the three clowns shared the same pitiful look.

"Yeah? Well, that's too bad," Squeaks said, cigarette dangling from the corner of his red lips. "Still, you should have called and let us know you would be late." He took off his curly blue wig and tossed it in his locker.

Harvey shook his head in disbelief. "Wow, you guys are real pals, aren't you? I bare my soul and tell you my wife is leaving me and you're all just, 'Oh, that's too bad, Harvey.'"

Squeaks slammed his locker door, making Harvey jump. "Makes sense. You're not much of a clown and an even worse business partner, so I doubt you're much of a husband."

Harvey's face burned beneath the pasty greasepaint. "What the hell did you just say, Barry?"

Pogo pushed Harvey back on his heels. "You know you've been letting this place down for years, Harvey," he said.

"We're always having to pick up your slack," Zany chimed in, stepping forward in his oversized clown shoes.

"You never do kids' parties," Squeaks added. "We always have to do them because all you want to do is the cancer kids."

"Those kids love me! And don't forget, I'm the one who

started this business and brought you in." Harvey poked Pogo in the chest.

"Love you?" Pogo laughed out loud. "You're just a fucking clown, not some thespian. Do you think your dancing and half-assed singing is gonna make those poor kids feel better? If I had cancer and had to listen to you, I'd be begging for the cancer to take me."

Harvey's right fist connected with Pogo's big red nose. It happened so fast that Harvey didn't realize what he'd done until he saw the blood on his knuckles.

"Oh, shit," was all he could say as he watched Pogo's large frame crash into one of the chairs.

Moments later, Squeaks and Zany launched themselves at Harvey, throwing wild punches of their own. Pain seared along Harvey's ribs and kidneys. A fist almost dislocated his jaw. Then Pogo was on his feet, screaming, and he came charging in to knock Harvey to the floor. He tasted blood mixed with greasepaint. He coiled into the fetal position, but the clowns were in a frenzy, tearing at Harvey's pinstripe suit with their bare hands.

"You're fucking mincemeat!" Pogo said.

Harvey was limp as they picked him up and hauled him toward the front doors. He felt a rush of air, and then the shattering of plate glass. He hit the pavement outside, his chin smacking against the concrete so hard he swallowed a tooth. Pieces of glass scraped his skin.

Through the haze of threatening unconsciousness, Harvey summoned the strength to get on his knees, and then stand. He staggered towards his car as Pogo's voice rang out behind him.

"I'm calling the cops on your ass, Harvey. Do you hear me? You're fucked!"

Giggles eased into the driver's seat of his car.

His entire body screamed in agony, and everywhere he looked he saw red. His happy face was splattered with blood in the rearview mirror, the white greasepaint beneath barely visible. Green and blue mascara had leaked into his eyes, turning them bloodshot. His smile was a wound, a long crimson arc across the bottom half of his face. When he grimaced, he saw that one of his front teeth was missing.

Giggles looked like a monster.

He tried to order his thoughts, but his skull only pounded in time with the hammering of his heart. He couldn't believe what was happening. Louisa had left him and his so-called friends and partners had insulted him and beaten him within an inch of his life. The day was like one bad joke.

Giggles spat blood out the car window. He was going to make them pay. He climbed out of the vehicle and moved to the trunk on unsteady feet. He grabbed the tire iron. He was going to cave Pogo's head in, and make him suffer. Make them all suffer.

Police sirens in the distance froze his rage. He had to run. If they caught him, they'd put him in a cage. Like a freak.

No, Giggles wouldn't have that.

He would live to fight another day.

Giggles drove to the first hardware store he could find. He weaved his car through the street, turning in front of oncoming traffic despite the honks of terrified drivers. He found a store—Dave's Hardware—and came to a screeching halt outside the front door.

The store was small, an out-of-the-way concrete cube on the corner, clearly forgotten in favor of the larger chain stores. Giggles just needed one thing. He grabbed the tire iron from the dash and shuffled inside.

There were two people in the store—a man at the counter looking to buy paint and the other, an older man, who Giggles presumed was the owner, Dave. Dave was probably two years short of retirement, Giggles figured. The other man was younger, roughly the same age as Giggles. The two men were rendered speechless by the sight of him.

"Do you sell guns here?" Giggles asked, but the *s* in *sell* came out like a whistle.

"Jesus Christ," the customer said. "What happened to you?" Then he chuckled. "And why are you dressed as a clown?"

Giggles ignored the customer and pulled the tire iron out from behind his back, pointing it at the old man.

"Do you sell guns?" Giggles asked again.

Dave held up his hands. "No...no I don't sell guns. There's a Winchester dealership about ten miles up the road. You could go there."

"Fuck." Giggles felt dizzy and let the iron fall to his side. He was too spaced out to drive anywhere else.

"Look, mister," the old man continued, "do you need me to call you an ambulance or something? You look like hell."

Giggles slammed the tire iron against the counter. "What I need is a fucking gun!"

The customer made for his phone, but Giggles swung the tire iron across his arm, the subsequent *crack* of bone and the man's scream echoing within the confines of the tiny store.

"Make a move, and I'll bash your brains in, got it?"

The customer whimpered at Giggles from the floor, his eyes wide with terror and pain.

"Nail gun!" Dave said.

Giggles turned to the old man. "What?"

"We uh...we have nail guns? In aisle three. Take one and leave...please!"

Dave was almost as white as Giggles' greasepaint. Would he have a heart attack? he wondered.

"Nail. Gun?" the clown said, considering whether it would be as effective as a gun to kill Pogo dead. He believed it would.

"Yes...in aisle three," Dave replied, pointing towards the center of the store.

Police sirens blared outside, and Giggles jumped to the doors. The cops had found him, tracking his car right to Dave's Hardware.

"Stupid! Stupid!" Giggles cursed. Quickly, he locked the doors and slid the tire iron between the door handles. Then, he turned and ran down aisle three—past the nail guns—to the back entrance. Beside it was a tall double-door refrigerator. Fueled by adrenaline, Giggles dragged it, grunting and pulling until it firmly blocked the only other way in or out.

A cry of pain drew Giggles back to the front counter where he found Dave tending to his wounded customer.

"His arm's broken," the old man told him. "He needs to go to a hospital."

Giggles tried to think, but another voice boomed from outside, "Mr. Dutton—this is the police. We know you are in there! We need you to come outside with your hands where we can see them!"

Giggles pulled off his wig and threw it to the floor. "No! No! No! No! No!"

"Hey, hey it's all right," Dave said. "Just stay calm, okay?"

"Don't fucking tell me to stay calm!"

The customer groaned, and Giggles was mesmerized by his arm's harsh angle.

"Come on, man…just let us go," the guy wheezed.

"Yeah, you do whatever you want," Dave said, "We don't care."

Giggles looked at the old man. "What did you say?"

Dave swallowed. "I-I just said you can do whatever you want. Just don't hurt us."

The clown thought of his wife and how this bad-day-turned-worse started with the mean things she said. He saw the customer's phone on the floor, the screen spiderweb-cracked. Giggles scooped it up.

"Can I use your phone?" But he was already dialing Louisa's number. He listened to the phone ringing on the other end, his eyes moving from Dave and his customer to the growing number of police officers in the parking lot and back again. He giggled.

Then, the call connected.

"Hello?" his wife said.

"Louisa, it's me. Please, don't hang up."

There was a long silence, then she said, "What do you want?"

"I-I just want to talk to you."

"Well, I don't want to talk to you."

"Please, Lou, listen to me. I know you're unhappy, and I'm sorry because I know it's my fault. I know you think I'm selfish, but I'm not. Everything I do is for us, for you. I like being a clown because, well…you have to make other people happy to be happy with yourself. I know it might seem silly to you, but people can't help but see me and smile."

There was an even longer pause before Louisa let out a heavy sigh.

"You're right, I am unhappy, but I also think you are, too. You just won't admit it to yourself. The clown, the makeup, it's all just masking the fact that we're both miserable and have been for a long time. Can't you see that?"

Giggles considered Dave and his customer again, seeing the terror and uncertainty in their eyes. He wasn't bringing smiles to their faces.

"I'm in real trouble," he said.

"Why?"

"Lou, I need to see you."

"No."

"Please."

"Have you done something? What did you do?

"Please, I need you."

The phone on the wall behind the counter rang, startling everyone in the room.

"Is that a phone?" Louisa said. "Where are you? Whose number are you calling me from?"

Giggles could see one of the officers on the phone through the glass doors, no doubt a negotiator to hear the crazy clown's demands. Giggles giggled as the phone kept ringing.

"Louisa, I'm sorry for disappointing you. I hope you find your happiness."

Giggles ended the call and let the phone clatter to the floor. There was nothing more to say. He stood there in Dave's Hardware, watching the officers outside scurry like rats. It was only a matter of time before they came crashing in, guns blazing. His plan seemed pointless now. His entire life.

It was time to send out the clown.

He thought of all the little boys and girls who would never discover his cheer, his whimsy. They'd go to their graves never meeting Giggles the Clown. Their faces flashed through his mind, particularly those who didn't win the fight. A thought occurred to him, and he reached into his trouser pocket and pulled out a packet of modelling balloons. All the balloons were black, ones he'd separated from all the other colors because dying kids didn't want to see black balloons. He giggled and began to fasten it into a shape.

"Wanna hear a joke?" he asked Dave.

The old man trembled, then forced a nod. "Uh…sure."

Giggles twisted the balloon into an L-shape and held it in his hand. He held the short part as a handle and the long part pointed towards the door.

"What do you call a problematic person with a gun?" Giggles said.

There was silence as Giggles watched the realization cross Dave's wrinkled face, eyes going wide. The old man knew what the object in Giggles' hand resembled. Still, he shrugged, understanding the punchline was coming.

The clown grinned, the bloody red smear of a smile creeping across his face. "A trouble-shooter."

Giggles the Clown walked to the door, pulled the tire iron free, and stepped outside, balloon-gun in hand, chuckling all the while.

# THIRTY YEARS LATER

### 30th October, 2024

Kelly Harris woke screaming.

She sat up, remembering she'd been on the couch, but not closing her eyes. The nightmare lingered in her mind, in her very soul. Dark entrances, a never-ending vista of shadowed trees, and the lifeless eyes of a young boy. The same boy she'd seen every night for thirty years.

Kelly wiped away the sweat from her brow, only for the tears to come. The painful realization that no matter what she did, no matter how many cups of coffee she drank, no matter how much she refused to sleep, the boy would always be there. To remind her of what she did.

What they all did.

"I can't do this anymore."

Kelly reached for her laptop and opened a new email message. She took a deep breath, urging her frantic heart to slow. It had been thirty years since that night, but twenty since she'd spoken to him, to any of them. Surely, she wasn't the only one suffering? She started typing with trembling fingers:

*Dear Dale,*

*I know it's been a long time. I don't even know if this is still your email.*

*I have to talk to you about that night. About what happened. Every night I dream about it. Do you dream about it too? I don't know how to get it to stop.*

*It's guilt. I know it is. You regret what happened, don't you? Maybe if we all admit our guilt the nightmare will stop…*

Kelly hovered the cursor over the SEND button, and stared at it for several minutes, agonized. The cavern's mouth, the boy's mouth click-clacked in her mind. She deleted the email.

Kelly knew the nightmare would not truly end unless she faced it head on.

Dale Dougherty had avoided Halloween for thirty years.

Two days before the holiday, he experienced the most vivid nightmare of his entire life, although he knew it wasn't a nightmare but a re-enactment. A revisitation of his youth, to a night he'd tried everything to forget.

The dream wrenched him from sleep, and he screamed. His shirt damp, he reached breathlessly for someone to save him, but there was no one, nothing that could help, only bundled bedsheets and the echo of his empty bedroom.

He sat on the edge of the bed, desperately trying to slow his heart and push the lingering threads of the nightmare from his head. The golden light of a new day broke through his curtains, and he was grateful to see it, thankful for anything other than the dark.

He shook beads of sweat from his close-cropped blond hair and grabbed the cigarette packet from the pocket of his jeans on the floor. He hadn't had a nightmare about Halloween 1994 for decades. He lit the cigarette and took a long drag. The smoke wafted about him, as did the nightmare's last remnants: masks, laughter, and a solitary scream.

Why was he dreaming about the kid? Why now, after all these years?

Dale slipped on his jeans, left the bedroom, and walked up the hallway to the kitchen of his small apartment. There were beer cans, an overflowing ashtray on the bench, and dishes in the sink. He saw a cockroach and squished it with the hot end of the cigarette, the insect releasing a hiss as it died. The sound reminded him of that night. Blinking the thoughts away, he filled the kettle and placed it on the stove. He was about to light another cigarette when he heard a knock at the door.

He looked through the peephole and saw a female uniformed police officer and a man in a suit—no doubt a detective—on his front porch. Dale slipped the chain lock back and opened the door. The detective was already holding up his gold shield.

"Detective Garrett Hedlund, Charlton PD. This is Officer Russell. Are you Dale Dougherty?"

Dale cleared his throat. "That's me. Is there something I can help you with, Officer?"

Hedlund put his ID back in his jacket. A chill breeze assailed the street, lifting the carpet of leaves on Dale's front lawn into the air. Across the street, Dale glimpsed a neighbor hammering fake headstones into his grass.

"Do you think we could come inside, Mr. Dougherty? We have something of importance to discuss with you."

Dale chuckled. "What's this about? Do I have some unpaid parking tickets or something?"

Hedlund smoothed his pencil-thin moustache, unimpressed. "Do you know a Maxwell Young?"

A cascade of images assaulted Dale's mind's eye. Fourteen-year-old Max, wearing a poorly made robot costume, crying in the woods.

"Uh…yeah, I know Max. But I haven't seen or heard from him since we left high school."

Hedlund nodded. "Well, I hate to be the one to tell you this, but Mr. Young was found murdered last night."

The contorted, shrieking face of a child slapped Dale's senses.

"Jesus… Murdered?"

"I'm afraid so. Again, Mr. Dougherty, can you invite us inside? There's a lot more to talk about."

Dale cleared the newspaper pages and television remote off the couch so the officers could sit. He thought of Max, dorky Max, with his love of *Star Wars* and *Voltron* and all that crap, dead, murdered. Dale sat opposite the officers in his weathered recliner and took a fresh cigarette from the packet.

"Do you mind if I…?" he asked them.

"Not at all," Hedlund said. "So, Mr. Dougherty, when was the last time you spoke to Max?"

"Oh, man. It was like '97 or '98, when we graduated high school."

"You two were close during school, though?"

"Definitely but, ah, I went straight into the Army when I finished high school. I'm not sure what Max ended up doing."

"What'd you do in the Army?" Hedlund asked.

"I was a Ranger."

"Thank you for your service," Officer Russell said.

Dale nodded and smiled. "Yeah…thanks."

Hedlund flipped through his notebook. "Uh, looks like Max got into IT, building computer systems. He worked for a firm in Charlton, but he was recently laid off."

Dale winced. "Oh, that's awful. A shame because I remember Max was great with computers, a real geek, you know?"

Hedlund took fresh notes as Dale talked and asked him a follow-up question without an upwards glance: "So, you grew up together, and lived in the same town, but you haven't spoken to him in decades?"

"That's right," Dale said.

"Then would you have any idea why the killer carved your name and that of several others into Max's body?"

Dale swallowed and put his cigarette out. "Carved?" He looked from Hedlund to Officer Russell.

"The killer cut several names into his chest," Hedlund continued. "His name, yours, Kelly Farris, and a Ryan McCammon."

A vision of Kelly dressed as a witch and Ryan as Superman flooded through.

"You know them as well, don't you, Mr. Dougherty?"

"They were…they were all my childhood friends."

Hedlund exchanged a look with his subordinate. "So, even though you all still live here in Charlton and were at school together for years, you've all lost touch? Why is that?"

Dale lit another cigarette and looked out the window to the street beyond—a street not unlike the one he and his friends walked that one Halloween night. The night that had haunted them all every night since.

## 31st October, 1994

Dale put on the cape and inserted the fake fangs into his mouth. "I vant to suck your blud!" he said in his worst Transylvanian accent.

Kelly Farris recoiled but laughed as Dale lunged comically for her throat. "Ah, get away!"

Dale smiled a vampiric smile. He knew Kelly was saying, "get away," but he knew she liked him—because he liked her, too. She looked so pretty in her long purple witch costume with pointed hat, all lace and taffeta, flowing in the chilly autumn breeze. He pulled his fangs free.

"Your costume looks great, Kell," he told her.

"Thanks. My mom spent hours sewing it."

"I can tell." Dale flared up the collar of his cape so that it framed his head. "What do you think of mine?"

Kelly looked him up and down. "If it wasn't for the cape and the fangs, you could be going to church."

"What? No, I'm Count Dracula!"

Kelly raised an eyebrow. "You don't say? Oh, yeah, you're right. I see it now!"

Dale gave her a playful shove, and they both burst out laughing. They were getting closer, there was no doubt about it. But Dale didn't want to come on too strong, so he turned away and looked to the street instead. Kids in white sheets, fairies and wolfmen mingled back and forth across the cul-de-sac, collecting candy. Carved pumpkins flickered with candlelight as the phrase "trick or treat" rang out into the night air. This was Halloween.

"Where are Max and Ryan?" Kelly asked with a slight scowl on her face.

"They said they'd be here by seven-thirty," Dale said.

Kelly pulled back one of her sleeves to study her watch. "Well, it's almost eight. My mom said I had to be back home by nine."

"I'm sure they'll be here soon, Kell."

"Wait!" Kelly pointed to two boys rounding a corner. "I see them!"

One boy, Max Young, was a shambling robot, the other a much

younger and skinnier version of Superman—Ryan McCammon.

"Wow, that has to be you under there, huh, Max?" Dale said.

"Yep, it's me!" His *robot*—a construction of cardboard boxes of varying sizes, decorated with tin foil and painted red, blue and gold—covered his arms, legs and torso. A large box on his head had a rudimentary drawing of a lion. "I'm Voltron!" he added.

"Sure, you are," Ryan said. "You just look like a big Lego."

"I do not!" Max protested.

"At least he put some effort in, unlike you, Super-Ryan," Dale said.

"Super-lame-Ryan more like it," Max added with a grin.

"Check out the spit curl!" Kelly said, flicking it with a finger.

Ryan put a hand over his face. "Don't touch it!"

The four of them laughed wildly, savoring the fun and joy of Halloween. The one night of the year when they could indulge and escape the monotony of their everyday lives.

"Okay, come on, you guys, let's get going," Dale said. "This candy isn't going to collect itself!"

They ran into the street, dodging the slow-moving cars and screaming toddlers. They knocked on a few doors and collected meagre amounts of candy, which only infuriated Ryan.

"It's all candy corn and marshmallows. Where are the chocolate bars?" he said.

"We'll do better at the next house," Kelly told him.

"No, we won't! Oh, man, this is just so crap. I knew I should have snuck into the movie to see that new Freddy Krueger movie that just came out. Would've made for a better Halloween night than this!"

Ryan kicked out at a pumpkin in the house's driveway. It exploded, sending a large chunk into the back of a standing skeleton statue, which toppled over and broke a Styrofoam headstone.

"Oh, shit!" Ryan said.

"Let's get outta here before the owner flips!" Max told them.

They ran, almost knocking over another group of trick-or-treaters. They reached the corner, huffing and puffing, but their fears quickly turned to new waves of laughter.

"Oh, man, what a rush!" Ryan said.

"Yeah, but let's not do that again," Dale told him, laughing.

"Yeah, yeah, keep your shirt on, Vlad," Ryan replied, but his attention was already turning back to the street. "Hey, isn't that that Barney kid—the retard?"

The others followed Ryan's gaze to a short, rotund boy in a red devil costume—red cape, red face, red pitchfork, and a matching red horned headband.

"Yeah, that's Barney Davis. He's a middle school kid," Max said.

"You shouldn't call him a retard, Ryan," Kelly scolded.

Ryan snickered. "Hah, look at him! Like he needs any more candy!"

"Ryan, come on, man," Dale said. "Let's get back to the trick-or-treating, okay?"

But Ryan ignored his friend and crossed the street to talk to Barney. The other kids followed, uncertain but curious about what Ryan was doing.

"Hey, Barney," Ryan said, startling the boy. "How's it going, man?"

"Uh, hello." Barney stopped to lean on his pitchfork.

Dale grabbed Ryan's cape. "Hey, what are you doing? Leave the kid alone."

Again, Ryan ignored him. "You got quite a lot of candy there, Barney."

"Yeah…"

"Not much of a scary Halloween, though, is it?"

Barney considered the revelers around him. "It's fun."

Ryan sidled up to the boy and put an arm around his shoulder. "Scary can be fun, too, though, right? It can be a real thrill."

Barney's red face gazed up at Ryan. "I guess."

Ryan pulled him closer and whispered in his ear, "Do you want to see something really scary?"

Charlton was a small town of almost ten thousand people, nestled in the center of a valley. A vast forest of great fir trees surrounded the town, dark and rising high into the night sky. That night, Ryan led his friends and Barney into those woods, searching for a good scare. They left the safety of the streetlights and the joy of Halloween to venture into a world much more sinister. The trees, black sentries against the violet night, waited to see what unfolded.

"I don't like this place," Barney said, but Ryan grabbed him by the shoulder.

"It's all okay. You're here with friends."

Barney considered Ryan and the others. "You're my friends?"

Ryan smiled at him. "Sure. We're all Barney's friends, right?"

Dale stopped as they entered an open area of the woods. The leaves crunched loudly beneath their shoes.

"Ryan, what are we doing here? We should get back."

Max took off his headwear. "Yeah, it's too dark, and I'm finding it hard to move."

"We should go home," Kelly said.

Ryan shook his head. "Don't be such a bunch of wusses. We're just gonna have some fun." He hugged Barney tight. "You're not scared, are you, Barney? Not like these guys."

Barney saw the trees. "It…it is kind of dark."

"It's all okay. You're safe with us. Now, listen, here's where it gets fun. Did you know there's supposed to be treasure buried here in these woods?"

Barney's red face turned to Ryan. "Treasure?"

"Yeah. Buried in an unmarked grave."

"Ryan, stop this," Dale said, and he reached out to grip his friend's arm, but Ryan jerked it away.

Dale looked at Barney, at how excited he was, but deep down he knew what Ryan was planning was a bad idea.

"I'm just having some fun with Barney here," he said through gritted teeth. "Some adventure. Like Indiana Jones. He lowered his voice and gazed back at Barney. "You like Indy, right?"

Barney chuckled nervously. "He was named after the dog!"

"Ha, that's right, he was! He liked the treasure, didn't he? He wasn't afraid to go into tombs to look for gold, so you shouldn't be either."

Ryan led Barney towards a large tree just off the beaten path. The others followed cautiously. "See, just over there, through those trees?" He crouched beside the boy to point. "There's an old cave. It's been there forever. They say there was a bank robber or a thief who stole a lot of money. He got shot and hid in there, but he died."

Kelly gripped Dale's hand. "Dale, you have to stop this," she said.

Dale moved to put a hand on Barney's back. "Come on, Barney, let's take you home."

Ryan pushed Dale back. "Hey, man, I'm just trying to have some fun."

"You're scaring him."

Barney shook his head. "No, I'm not scared."

Ryan smiled. "See? He's not scared. He's not afraid of going into the cave to find the treasure."

"I'll do it," the boy added and, before anyone could reply, he ran off toward the cave.

"No, Barney, wait!" Dale urged.

Ryan pushed his friend again. "Leave it!"

"You're an idiot. You don't know what's in that cave. He could fall or—"

"That kid's braver than you. You don't even have the guts to tell Kelly you like her, but Barney just ran into a dark cave without a second thought."

Dale's cheeks burned suddenly, and he couldn't meet Kelly's gaze, even though she stood right next to him. "If Barney's hurt, I'll—"

Dale's reply was cut short by a high-pitched scream. It echoed from the cave and out into the woods, radiating through the teenagers' very bones, chilling them.

"Oh, shit," Dale said. "Barney!"

They all ran towards the cave through the thick undergrowth. Even in the dark, Dale could discern the entrance to the cave, like a gaping maw. Yet, it was what lay outside the cave that terrified them even more.

Barney was on the ground, coiled up in rigor; a cadaverous spasm like an invisible flame had claimed him. His hands were contorted, framing a face stretched into an unnatural scream.

When Kelly shrieked at the sight, it was as if Barney screamed his last breath all over again.

## 30th October, 2024

"What happened to Max, Detective Hedlund?" Dale said. Hedlund and Officer Russell exchanged a knowing glance, and when neither of them replied, Dale insisted. "You said the killer carved my name and the names of my friends into Max's chest. You said he was murdered. But could he have...done it to himself?"

The suggestion turned Hedlund's gaze. "Why would you say that, Mr. Dougherty?"

Dale shrugged. "I-I don't know. You said Max lost his job. Could he have been depressed?"

"The autopsy determined his wounds weren't self-inflicted. There were no hesitation cuts."

Dale lit a new cigarette. "So, were the knife marks—the name-carving—what killed him?"

"No, it appears he was strangled," Hedlund said. "But his face..."

Dale recalled Barney's silently shrieking visage. "His face? What about his face?"

"His face was frozen in a scream. He was also wearing..." Hedlund raised an eyebrow in consternation, "a devil horn headband, and his face was painted with blood. Does that mean anything to you, Mr. Dougherty?"

"Jesus, no." Dale tried to keep his concern from showing. Hedlund stood.

"Do you know of anyone who might have had a grievance with Mr. Young, or you or your friends? Anything perhaps from your younger days?"

"No...we never got into any real trouble," Dale said. A cascade of images. Barney's mouth frozen in terror. Almost a copy of the cave.

The detective put his notebook away and handed Dale his business card. "Well, I suggest that you give those possibilities some serious thought. Whoever this killer is, they might be looking to target you all. Stay home if possible, and keep your home locked at all times."

Dale got out of his chair and followed them to the door. His fingers, slick with sweat, struggled to find purchase on the handle for a moment. He prayed the officers didn't notice. "No problem."

"Also, if you think of anything else, don't hesitate to call me."

An hour later, Dale got in his truck and drove to the edge of town, a place he hadn't visited for thirty years.

He knew the path so well he could have walked it blindfolded. It was the place where so many childhoods died, including Barney Davis's.

The setting sun cast shards of fading light between the fir trees. The cold was so palpable he could almost see it. He stood in the open field space of the woods, which now featured a bench and chairs and an outdoor barbecue. The entire area looked like it was dying, too, depleted of all color. It was grey and listless, with hardly a leaf on the ground. Dale had just located the cave and considered moving closer when a voice brought him to a standstill.

"I had a feeling you'd come here."

Dale turned and saw a tall, sandy-haired woman staring at him. He softened when he realized who she was.

"Kelly?"

She offered him a small smile. "Fancy seeing you here, Dale."

He walked to her, and they shared an embrace, but Kelly felt stiff in his arms, tense.

"Hey," he said, looking her in the eye. She was even more beautiful thirty years on. "What are you doing here, Kell?"

Kelly took a step back. "I would ask you the same thing, but I'm sure we're both here for the same reason."

Dale slipped his hands into his pockets. "You heard about Max, too, from the cops?"

"I saw them this morning. They spoke to you, then?"

"Yeah, what did they tell you?"

Kelly looked up at the trees. "That someone killed him. That I might be next."

Dale chuffed a shoe in the dirt and scratched the back of his head. "I can't believe this is happening. I mean, it can't be, can it?"

She folded her arms. "Did someone in Barney's family find out what happened here that night?"

"I never told anyone, not even my folks, and they went to the grave not knowing. Besides, the cops and the coroner all ruled the kid's death was a freak heart attack. Natural causes."

Kelly flashed him a look of contempt. "Nothing about Barney's death was natural causes, Dale. You saw his face." She paused, her expression suddenly pained. "It's haunted me ever since."

"As it has me, Kell. So, how the hell did Max get killed? Who knows?"

She threw her hands in the air and walked in circles in the dirt. "Maybe Ryan knows who it is?"

"Ryan? Last I heard, he was in jail for drug trafficking or overdosed."

His friend went and sat at the picnic bench, and Dale could tell the conversation was wearing her down. "If he is alive, then the cops will want to talk to him. I think that detective's going to figure out it has something to do with Barney." She rubbed her temples. "What if they reopen the investigation?"

Dale sat opposite her and reached for her hands, only she pulled away. "If they do, it'll be Ryan who ends up in trouble, Kell, not us."

She scowled at him. "Are you kidding me? We covered it up. We lied to the cops that night, told them Barney just keeled over and died."

"Because that's what happened. We didn't kill him."

Kelly looked past him, over Dale's shoulder at the cave. "The story Ryan told Barney about the cave, about the thief. Was that true?"

"Just an urban legend," he said, shrugging. "Some crap made up a century ago to scare kids."

Dale watched her bite her fingernails. He wanted to comfort her, but their rift had remained strong even after so many years.

"Something scared him to death, Dale," she said finally.

"What? A ghost? Kell, there's no such thing."

"Maybe we created one when Barney died."

Dale chuckled. "You can't be serious."

She leaned in close. "What if it's Barney? What if his ghost came back to take revenge on Max and we're next?"

## 31st October, 2024

Ryan's hunger for a fix always seemed to be at its fiercest come twilight.

He shuffled through Charlton's darkened streets and alleyways, scanning the equally haggard faces around him for the one with the *look*. The nobody who could give him what he craved. He walked past one sleeping beside a dumpster, almost tripping on a cluster of empty beer bottles. It was cold tonight, deathly cold, and the alley's brick walls were slick with the beginnings of the frost yet to come.

Leaning against one of those walls, Ryan pulled a scrunched packet of cigarettes from his pocket and lit the only one left. It would have to do until he got that next hit. When it finally became dark, he hoped that more nobodies would come out to play.

A gaggle of laughter made Ryan turn. A group of kids walked by, dressed in brightly colored costumes. He could make out that one of them wore a wolfman mask as they passed.

"Halloween," Ryan said to himself. "It must…be Halloween."

Ryan remembered that Halloween a long time ago, not the exact details, and he'd decided never to celebrate the holiday again. Around the same time, he tried taking more risks—stealing cars, breaking into houses, doing drugs, and then dealing them. It all started after *that* Halloween.

"Fuck off, you trick-or-treaters!" he screamed into the alley. He knew the kids were long gone, but it still felt good to say it. "Fuck off, Halloween!"

Ryan chuckled to himself and slipped off the wall, landing in the detritus of the alley. He laughed at his clumsiness. As he got up, he saw a young boy and a man watching him.

"What the fuck are you looking at?" Ryan asked, but they didn't move along, just kept on observing. Ryan got up and rushed towards them. "You think this is some kind of peep show?"

The boy wore a red cape, a red headband with horns on top, and carried a red pitchfork. Even the boy's face was painted bright red, and the more Ryan looked at that face, the more familiar it became. The man standing behind the boy was less evident, harder for Ryan to distinguish in his inebriated state. The man seemed intangible, as if made from nothing but air.

Ryan stepped closer, his eyes trying to get a better fix on the boy's face. He knew he'd seen it before—thirty years ago.

"B-Barney?"

The child replied with a loud and long scream that split his mouth at the corners, releasing a torrent of blackish fluid.

All Ryan could do was scream right along with him.

Kelly strode back to her car, Dale in tow.

"Kell, wait! You really can't be serious about this ghost crap!"

She unlocked the car and got in the driver's seat, but Dale reached out to keep her from closing the door.

"Let go, Dale!"

"Kell, this is ridiculous. Barney died of fright."

"Then who murdered Max, huh? The police told me someone carved our names on his chest. Clearly, someone knows the truth."

Dale rubbed the stubble on his face. "Okay, look, maybe there was someone else in the woods that night who saw us. Maybe they killed Max."

Kelly scoffed. "Then why didn't they go to the cops that night, or any other time in the last thirty years for that matter?!"

"I don't know, but it sounds more plausible than Barney's ghost!"

"Something scared Barney to death, something in that cave, and we let it happen. I'm not going to sit around waiting for whatever it is to get me. And you shouldn't either!"

Kelly pulled the door free and slammed it closed. In a huff, she started the car and drove off at speed, leaving Dale in a cloud of dust. She hoped she'd never see him again. All that mattered now was that she protected herself from the evil seeking her out.

Dale kicked the dirt, frustrated that Kelly wasn't listening to reason. He didn't know who had murdered Max, but Kelly's ghost theory was absurd, and he was going to prove it.

He went to the glovebox of his truck and retrieved his tactical flashlight. Behind him, the forest of fir trees loomed high, their peaks like blackened teeth, biting the night. He flicked on the flashlight, and it cast a long white beam into the woods. Dale wasn't going to let some ghost story get in the way of the truth.

The flashlight darted left and right across the undergrowth, green ferns and leaves appearing and disappearing in and out of the black. Moss and creeper vines had taken over the cave entrance in the past thirty years, but its mouth still dominated the rock face, inviting strangers to venture inside. His flashlight illuminated the interior, painting over the craggy surface and casting deep shadows, but Dale kept moving in, eager to know who was behind Max's death. After several minutes of searching, Dale had found nothing but rocks and dirt. There were no markings on the walls, no skeletons trapped under fallen boulders.

"It's just a cave," he said, and his voice bounced around the cave and back to him. "What the hell were you so afraid of, Barney?"

A scraping sound made Dale turn. The *tick-tack-tack* of pebbles falling. He cast his flashlight upon every wall surface.

"Who's there?" Dale wouldn't admit he was scared, but his heart told him otherwise. "Come out, you son of a bitch!"

He swung the beam about, and it passed over a shape, a figure swathed in red. Even thirty years on, the figure's identity was unmistakable.

"Jesus Christ! Barney?" he staggered back, almost losing his footing on the craggy floor of the cave. Kelly was right all along. Dale was looking at the ghost of Barney Davis.

The dead boy's red face was stark in the beam of light, but the boy seemed not to be affected by it. He didn't even blink. Yet, his lips moved as if he was trying to say something.

"What?" Dale said, stepping closer. "What are you saying? I can't hear you."

Barney's lips kept moving. Dale stared at them, trying to decipher what he whispered. Lip-reading was something he'd tried to master in the Army, watching insurgents scheming from a distance through a scope, but it wasn't a skill he'd perfected. Still, he managed to get two words:

*Kelly.*

*Grave.*

Dale blinked, and Barney vanished.

"Wait! What about Kelly?"

He scanned the cave, but there was no sign of the ghost. Dale didn't know what he'd experienced inside the cave, but he was sure of one salient fact:

Kelly was in grave danger.

Thirty years after he died, Kelly visited Barney Davis's grave for the first time.

Visiting Barney on Halloween felt wrong, but the idea of standing before his headstone had always terrified her. Kelly and the other children could have attended the boy's funeral back in 1994, but none had. How this never raised suspicion back then, Kelly didn't know, but now, thirty years later, she was finally taking steps to correct a mistake.

Barney's headstone was grimy, streaked with greenish-black mould, and Kelly noticed the others around it were slightly less so. There were flowers on the boy's grave, but they were old. She surmised the boy's parents were probably in their seventies or eighties now, too old and frail to relive such a tragedy. Or perhaps they'd moved far away to help them forget. That, Kelly realized, was what she should have done, but there was no escaping the guilt. Especially not now.

"Hello, Barney," she said to the headstone.

The night was young—Halloween night. A chill wind was building, scattering orange and red leaves over the cemetery like falling tears. Kelly shed tears of her own.

"I'm here because I wanted to say…I'm sorry, Barney. What Ryan did, what we all did to you that night back in the woods was wrong. Completely wrong. We took advantage of you and, for that, I am sorry. I know it probably doesn't mean anything but…I just wanted to say it. Right here and now. And I wanted you to hear it from one of us."

The wind whistled in reply, sending more autumn leaves swirling around her. She crouched and ran her fingers over the etched letters of Barney's name.

"What was it that scared you that night? What was it that made you come back?"

Kelly sighed and observed the cemetery with its grey headstones in rows and rows heading off into the distance. As she looked, a movement caught her eye, a shape watching her. She gasped.

The thing appeared to be a man comprised of grey, naked flesh. Its skin was translucent, showing the bones beneath. Mortified, Kelly was locked to the spot, unable to turn away as the thing's face twisted and morphed into other faces—all of them screaming. Kelly backed away when the specter suddenly crossed the space between them to hover over Barney's grave. Kelly shrieked and toppled backward, striking her shoulder on another headstone.

"Oh, my God!"

Dazed and in pain, Kelly looked up as the ghost peered at her. Its face changed again and again, in a sickening loop, and Kelly recognized every one. The faces belonged to Max Young, Ryan McCammon, and Barney Davis. All of them red with blood. She held up her hands to defend herself when the ghost lunged forward to show its true face.

"It's you…isn't it?" Kelly gasped. "The thing from the cave. The long-dead thief?"

The wraith hissed in reply.

"You scared Barney to death and, somehow…that set you free. Then you scared Max and Ryan, too…"

A gunshot rang out, and small fragments of damaged

headstone struck Kelly. She turned to see Dale with a gun, wide-eyed, looking at her in disbelief and fear. Fear for her safety.

"Dale," she said.

"Run!" he shouted.

Kelly screamed and scrambled to her feet to hide behind a large oak tree. The unnatural wind tore through the cemetery and tossed up a new swarm of leaves. Heart pounding, Kelly stared in horror as Dale tossed his useless gun away. The wraith leapt onto him, and his screams filled Kelly's ears as it drained him, turning him into a lifeless husk. His body fell in a twisted heap amongst the headstones.

Then the wraith looked Kelly's way. She screamed again and made to run, but the thing released an agonized shriek of its own. She braved a look over her shoulder. Above the cemetery, the collective ghosts of her friends ripped the wraith apart. The victims were fighting back.

Dale, Max and Ryan pulled at the thing's arms and tore at its chest, all in a bid to keep Kelly safe. In turn, they were breaking down their own spiritual bonds, the pieces of them glowing threads of light that became thinner by the moment. Kelly glimpsed one more visage through the blinding display—that of Barney Davis.

He offered Kelly one final smile before joining the fray.

The wraith released a booming howl that knocked Kelly to the ground. When the sound and light faded, she realized the wraith—and her friends—were gone.

Thirty years later, Kelly, Dale, Max, and Ryan were finally forgiven.

# MIDNIGHT MASQUERADE

The six sat in a circle in the hall, silently glancing at one another and wondering, waiting for the first person to speak. The expressions of the group mirrored hers—a mask of anxiety. A small table stacked with Styrofoam coffee cops and equally tasteless coffee sat in one corner of the echo-filled space. Emma's gaze had wavered between that table and the one vacant chair in the room, the one for their counsellor. After many painful moments of silence, she breathed a sigh of relief when he hurried into the room.

"Sorry I'm late everyone. Traffic was horrendous," said the counselor. He sat, gathered his clipboard, and began. "Thanks everyone for coming, especially the newcomers. It's a brave step you've taken, and I want to assure you that you'll only find support and guidance here, not judgment. The Victims of Crime Association helps thousands of people each year, and you should feel proud to be among them. Before we get started, my name is Steve, and I am the coordinator for this branch. I've been with the VCA for almost six years, and I originally started right where you are now—as a victim of crime. But my story isn't as important as yours right now, so please know this is a safe space. Feel free to say as much or as little as you like."

The group remained silent, and Emma took a moment to study their faces. She was surprised by the differences in age, but each carried that same look of shame.

"So..." said Steve. "Would anyone like to start things off?"

The man to Emma's left raised his hand. In his mid-forties, he was stout, had a thick beard, and wore thick-framed glasses. His gaze shifted nervously from person to person.

"Go ahead and introduce yourself," said Steve.

"Um, hi everyone—my name is Martin. Martin Adams."

The group said in unison: "Hi, Martin."

Martin cleared his throat. "Um…I live in Birchfield, just outside the city, and uh…"

"Take your time," said Steve. Emma wasn't sure if he was being sincere.

Martin nodded and continued. "Yeah, so um about uh, eighteen months ago my fiancé, Rachel was, um…working late in the city. She uh…worked as a pathologist, which meant that sometimes she had to do shift work and late-night call-outs, you know? Um, anyway, she finished late one night and was walking to her car when—"

He abruptly burst into sobs, his large frame bobbing up and down with each snuffling cry. Emma was uncomfortable sitting so close to a grown man crying.

"It's okay, Martin," said Steve. "We're here for you."

Martin wiped the tears from his tired eyes. "This guy…well he went for Rachel's purse, you know? The guy…was an addict…or a dealer. My Rachel…she uh…she tried to fight him off but…but he…he had a knife and—"

The man began to heave great sobs. Emma couldn't help but imagine the attacker stabbing Rachel over and over. The scene brought forth horrors from beneath the surface of her subconscious, where they always lurked, waiting for the right moment—the leering face and the foul smile.

"Okay," said Steve. "We might take a break if that's okay with everyone—so we can let Martin regain his composure? But Martin, thank you so much for sharing. It was brave of you. Okay, everyone, let's meet back here in ten minutes."

Emma noticed an easing of tension in the room. The others seemed relieved to have moved past the initial introduction phase and Steve seemed competent and understanding—Emma saw him go to Martin to offer further advice and comfort. Comfort wasn't what Emma was looking for right now. What she needed was to escape—her emotions, her thoughts—everything.

Emma puffed on her cigarette, trying to push back memories of that night, but her trembling fingers reminded her it was pointless. Instead, she focused on the passing traffic and the people walking and talking. How many of them shared her trauma? How many of them had imperfect lives?

A man watching her from across the street caught her eye. Immediately she dropped her cigarette on the ground and moved to quickly re-enter the VCA building when he braved the traffic to cross the street in her direction. Emma gasped when he addressed her directly.

"You know, you're wasting your time in there."

He was so close that Emma could see a lip piercing and skull cheek tattoo. Scraggly black hair obscured his eyes. He held up his hands.

"I'm not gonna hurt you, so chill, all right?"

Emma's heart pounded in her ears. The images of the leering face resurfaced. She wanted to scream.

"I can help you, you know," said the stranger.

"I-I don't have any money."

He shook his head, threads of hair shifting to reveal blue eyes. "You're a victim, right? You wouldn't be here otherwise."

Emma's eyes widened. "I don't know what you—"

"I can help you. Way more than just sitting around and talking about your feelings."

Emma fell mute, the experiences of that night threatening.

"I can help you get the guy who did it."

"W-What?"

"I know you're a victim; I can see it in your eyes. In the way you carry yourself. The guilt and the shame are like chains around your neck."

The scream sat at the back of her throat. The tears came first, and she started to shake. The man took a step back and offered her a business card.

"I know a way to help you," he said, "I was a victim once, but not anymore. Come to this address if you want to learn more."

Shaken, Emma went back inside to the meeting. She wanted to tell someone what happened, maybe even call the police, but the stranger's words burned a hole in her mind until the session ended.

Once outside and away from prying eyes and ears, she took out the card to study it. It was a thick card embossed with an address: *1606 Mason Court*. The high quality of the card didn't match the roughness of its provider. Was it a trap, a lure to get her alone? She scratched the edge of the card with a thumbnail, confusion rising alongside the fear. How could the stranger have guessed her secret torment? She'd never seen him before at any VCA meeting. What so-called help was waiting for her at 1606 Mason Court?

Martin passed her on the stairs. She reached out for the sleeve of his coat, startling him.

"I didn't mean to frighten you," she said. "I…well, I just wanted to talk to you."

"To me? What about?"

"Just um…I just wanted to say how sorry I am about what happened to your fiancé—Rachel."

Martin looked like he would cry again, until he offered Emma a smile. "Thank you," he said. "That means a lot."

Emma nodded. "I know how hard it can be to share our stories with total strangers."

Martin took off his glasses and wiped them with a handkerchief. "Yeah. Sometimes I wonder why it happened, you know… Why her?"

"I wonder the same thing—every day."

He replaced his glasses. "I'd take it back if I could."

Emma fingered the card in her pocket. The stranger's words lingered. "Did you ever find out who did it?"

Martin shook his head. "The police found nothing."

"Imagine if there was a way to find out."

He frowned. "What do you mean?"

She looked over her shoulder and stepped closer to him. "What if you had the chance to get the guy?"

Martin's mouth hung open. "Are you joking? 'Cause that's not funny…"

She toyed with whether to show Martin the card. "I'm sorry. I just had a weird experience before. This guy…came up to me from the street. He told me he knew how to find the asshole who—" She swallowed. "Who *assaulted* me."

Martin softened. "Oh, my god, were you…?"

Emma shrank from the question.

Martin stiffened and began to ramble. "Look, don't take this the wrong way…but I found it really difficult to tell my story tonight and I'm not sure that uh…that I'll be coming back. I'm sorry about what happened to you. I hope you can find the help you need. I'm sorry."

Emma didn't know why but she took a cab straight to Mason Court. She stood on the kerb across the street and stared at its façade. Number 1606 was a turn-of-the-century building wedged between two modern apartments. The brickwork was weathered, grey and cracked, while the surrounding streetlights seemed to draw out the shadows rather than diminish them. Seven stone steps led to an ornate front door of heavy oak, painted black.

Emma checked the address on the business card and then looked more carefully at the building. Every instinct told her to drop the card and run.

"I once stood where you are now."

Emma released a cry at the sound of the stranger's voice.

Again, he held up his hands in mock surrender. "Okay, sorry, you know I don't mean to scare you."

"Well, you keep coming out of nowhere!"

"Yeah, I guess it's been my thing for a long time." He took out a pack of cigarettes and offered her one, but she shook her head. "You smoke, right? I mean, I saw you on the street with one."

She pointed the card at him. "Who the fuck are you? Why did you give me this card and what…"—she gestured to the old building—"what exactly is that place?"

He lit up, took a long drag, and exhaled. "My name is Dixon. You know why I gave you that card? That place is your salvation."

"My salvation?"

Dixon flicked the fringe out of his eyes. "I think the more important question you need to be asking yourself is what made you decide to come here."

Emma turned to the building. "I-I don't know."

Dixon took another drag and tossed the cigarette away. "You want to know *how* I know."

She turned back to him. "Yes."

"It's this place. It knows. And it told me to come and find you, offer you an invitation."

"To get the…the piece of shit who did this to me? How? I don't even know who he is. All I have are fucking nightmares about a face I can't remember. The cops have no idea who he is, so how could *you*?"

Dixon shrugged. "As I said, it's not me. It's that place. All I know is that I got the salvation I wanted when I walked through those doors."

"How? How did it help you?"

He put his hands in his pockets and leaned against the wall, his gaze on 1606 Mason Court. He sighed like he was tired.

"My little brother and I got into a lot of trouble when we were kids and ended up in juvie. The warden and his goons were the worst of the worst. They beat my brother and me every night. Every fucking night. We were in the place for nearly five years. In the end, my little brother took so many beatings that it fucked with his head. Left him a fucking vegetable. I had to be the one to shut him off. I eventually got released and tried to live a normal life, but every day, I would think of my little brother and how I wanted to get the fuckers who killed him. Then, one day, this guy comes up to me and gives me the same card you're holding now."

Emma looked down at the card. Dixon stepped closer.

"Come across the street with me, and I promise that I'll show you how I got my life back…and how you can too."

After Dixon opened the front door to 1606 Mason Court, he led Emma down a darkened hallway that ended with another door.

Trepidation set her heart pounding, but she felt there was no turning back, she was committed to learning the secret. Light glimmered softly around the edges of the second door and as she and Dixon approached, it opened of its own accord. Dixon looked over his shoulder and gave her a broad smile.

"Pretty freaky, huh?"

Emma followed him and they stepped across the threshold into a circular room. On the wall in front of them were rows of small drawers, like safety deposit boxes. The brass locks on the drawers seemed to shine.

"What is this place?" said Emma.

Dixon pressed a finger to his lips and reached out a hand for the card. He took it towards the wall of drawers. A lock opened with a click, and one of the drawers in the center row slowly slid open.

"Candidate Emma Walker," said Dixon.

"How did you know my—" whispered Emma, but again Dixon silenced her.

He placed the card inside the drawer, and it retracted, closing with a soft scrape. A moment passed and all Emma could do was breathe and listen to the beat of her terrified heart. She considered turning and running out the door but the entry had already closed. A further scraping sound made her turn back to see the drawer had reopened. Dixon stepped forward and retrieved what she thought was the same card—until he handed it to her. On the card was the new printed text:

*Rick Miller, 1289 Brighton Street.*

She read the text and looked at Dixon. "What is it?"

"That's your chance," he told her.

Emma stared at the text, the name *Rick Miller* burning into her subconscious. The leering face that had haunted her—scarred her—now had a name. The text began to blur as tears welled in her eyes.

"This…this is him?"

Dixon nodded. The scraping returned; another drawer had opened beside the first. Dixon gestured for Emma to approach it.

"You have to be the one to take it," he said.

She wiped the tears from her eyes and cautiously went to the drawer. At first, she thought the drawer contained only darkness. She leaned in closer. The contents made her gasp. Inside was a mask. It was flesh but devoid of any facial features. It was simply a blank human visage, both blind and mute. She picked it up and faced Dixon.

"What the fuck is going on? What is this?"

"It's anonymity."

"What?"

He pointed to the open drawer. "It's part of the deal. They give you the means—and the tools—to get the justice you deserve."

Emma scanned the wall and the ceiling. The drawers seemed to disappear into the darkness.

"They? Who are *they*? What's behind this wall?" She held out the card. "How the fuck do they know who he is?"

Dixon pushed a strand of hair aside. "There's no point asking these questions. They just know. And I swear to you that it's all true. They gave me what I wanted and they can give it to you too. All they ask is that you wear the mask so they can watch."

Emma scoffed. "Watch me what?"

He looked at the card and then into Emma's eyes. "Come on, Emma—so you can *kill* him."

The name *Rick Miller* was stark against the perfect white card. The thought of killing the man responsible had always resided in the deepest recesses of her heart.

"Take the mask," Dixon said. "Take it and that card and get what you deserve."

Brighton Street was in the projects, the lost part of the city. Emma took the 12.05am bus, staring out the window to watch the streets gradually become darker, filthier, and more desperate. On the journey, she thought about how desperate *she* was—how far she would go.

She got off the bus at 1261, deciding to walk the rest of the way. Her destiny was only a block away. She walked past the homeless and downtrodden, counting the house numbers. The items in her jacket pockets weighed heavily on her mind.

Then 1289 Brighton Street came into view on a corner. The house was a single-story timber shack with peeling paint and a front lawn of dying grass. A chain-link fence surrounded it, but the front gate was wide open. Through the front window she glimpsed a figure bathed in the flickering light of a television.

Emma checked over her shoulder to make sure no one was around, she retrieved the mask from her left jacket pocket. When she held the mask the first time, it was cool to the touch; now it felt warm in her hands. She turned it over and saw the inside of the mask was still pitch black. She wondered how she was going to see out of it.

"Anonymity," she whispered.

She placed the mask over her face and a pulse immediately spread throughout her body as if she had suffered an electric shock. Confusion reigned as a cacophony of voices entered Emma's head. Her vision turned blood-red, and the taste of metal flooded her tongue. A wave of compulsion washed over her, and she could only watch herself as she started to walk through the front gate of 1289 Brighton Street and up the steps. Her right hand moved on its own to knock on the door. The voices rang in her head.

*You wanted this.*

*This is what you asked for.*

Emma reached into her right pocket and pulled out the gun.

*This is what you want.*

*This is what we want.*

Rick Miller opened his front door. The leering face—the mask that plagued her dreams, her future.

Emma raised her hand and squeezed the trigger.

Emma's clothes smelled like Rick Miller's blood. She re-entered the house at 1606 Mason Court, the doors swinging open to welcome her, but at that moment, she wanted to be somewhere else, anywhere else.

She walked into the circular room, her legs shaking so much she could barely manage it. There was no one else in the room, no Dixon—only her and the wall of featureless drawers. She took off the mask and the fifth drawer in the center row crept open. She reached into her right pocket and took out the gun, which still reeked of its last act. A second drawer opened. She looked at the open drawers like judgemental eyes and released a long scream. The sound cascaded through the room, serving to remind her she was alone.

"You made me do that!" she said to the wall. "You made me no better than him!"

Emma waited, expecting a response, but the drawers sat open, like a pair of hungry hands.

"Why? Why did you give me this?"

When no reply came, Emma tossed the mask and the gun away and scrambled to the wall to pull the drawers until they came free, leaving two rectangular wounds. She dropped to her knees and screamed into the dark holes.

"Answer me! Who the fuck are you?"

Again came silence, which only fuelled her rage. She pulled out another drawer and another. She looked into each hole, finding only darkness on the other side, until glints of light appeared. Faces-masks tethered to the black. They were the same mask she'd worn when she murdered Rick Miller. She had been wearing *them.*

*We know what lies behind men's faces, behind their souls.*

Emma sobbed. "You…you made me kill him. So that you could fucking watch?"

*Sin is sin. Punishment is punishment.*

"Then why do I feel like you're punishing *me?*" Emma slammed her fist on the wall. "What are you—angels, demons? All I see are faceless fucking freaks! How can you do this to people?"

The masks retreated into the dark, leaving behind only the echo of one final refrain.

*We gave you a choice: either salvation or damnation. It's how you chose.*

Emma waited for Martin on the stairs outside the Victims of Crime Association building. When he emerged, she could tell by his eyes that he'd been crying, that he was still having nightmares about

Rachel and the man who had taken her from him. He saw her and stopped halfway down the stairs.

"Emma—wow. Nobody's seen you in weeks."

She offered him a smile. "You know you're wasting your time in there."

Martin adjusted his glasses as she handed him a business card.

"They can't help you," she said. "But I can."

# LEFT ON OCTOBER LANE

Jake sat on the end of the bed in his skeleton onesie listening to a real-life monster screaming at his mum, the horrible sound echoing throughout the house.

Twenty minutes before, his stepdad John had come home smelling of drink, lumbering beast-like into the kitchen demanding his steak and beer. Jake had been watching TV, staring at Laurie Strode's terrified gaze when John had walked in. John's stern voice had drawn Jake's gaze to his mother. Laurie Strode's look of fear didn't even compare. Mother and son's eyes met and when John noticed, he'd stepped between them.

"Hey, I'm talking to you," John told Shelley.

"I'm sorry," she'd replied, and Jake couldn't help but wish she was holding a knife, like Laurie on the TV.

John staggered over to stare at Jake and what he was watching. He laughed and shook his head.

"What in the name of Christ have you got this kid watching now, Shelley?"

Jake averted his stepdad's gaze and watched Michael Myers' pale face dominate the screen; he so wanted to be as strong as Michael. John's voice soared with each vile word that passed his lips.

"How can you let a twelve-year-old watch that crap, Shelley? You're letting him rot his god-damned mind—do you know that?"

John stormed across the lounge room and switched off the TV with such force that it almost toppled over.

"Get your ass in your room, boy," John said.

"Please John, leave him, it's Halloween—he just wants to watch one movie..."

Jake could tell his mother knew she had made a mistake and her voice trailed off, but there was no doubt that John had heard her. A wave of fury filled his eyes, more terrifying than any celluloid serial killer.

"What did you say to me?"

John defied his inebriation to move like a ghost into the kitchen. The following harsh slap of skin on skin that rang out was like a starter's pistol and it sent Jake out of the lounge room and down the hall so fast that he thought hell was on his heels.

As John's tirade had filled the house, Jake had donned his costume and took solace in the mirror, imagining that it was his reflection that was feeling the pain and crying the tears.

Those terrible twenty minutes had felt like a lifetime, his tiny heart trapped in a dungeon of fear. All he wanted to do was escape into the street—into Halloween. He'd take fake horrors over real ones any day. If only Billy was still home. His big brother was the only one who seemed able to stand up to John. But Billy was long gone and Jake and Shelley were alone, at the mercy of the monster.

Jake looked at his bedroom window. He could sneak out; scale the drainpipe and jump down onto the carpet of leaves below. He'd follow the laughs of happier children all the way to the kerb, run away from his fear.

And before he could give it a second thought, he did just that.

The street was painted in velvet twilight, the day making way for Halloween Night. Jake felt the chill air through his costume and he quickly pulled the hood over his head. He should have grabbed a coat, but it was too late; he wouldn't dare go back into that house now. Without even a look over his shoulder he ran to the kerb and made a sharp left turn towards the sounds of Halloween.

The last night of October became more prevalent with each step, front porches were decorated with candlelit pumpkins and cardboard ghosts and princesses, aliens and superheroes stood on every corner, seeking out candy. It was as Jake observed the other children that he realized he hadn't grabbed a basket or bag to collect any candy either, but deep down he knew he really wanted to savor the freedom, not knock on the doors of unknown houses. He stopped running and took in the sights and sounds. He knew he was doing the wrong thing, but he didn't care. He couldn't help his mother, she could only help herself. As he observed the darkening street, Jake felt a stab of anger when John's face filled his mind's eye. He'd never hated someone so much before. If only the slob would just go away… If only he'd just drop dead. Jake clenched his fists, the nails digging deep into his palms. If only he was older, he'd kill John himself.

Jake stood in the street and took deep, calming breaths. He'd never had such thoughts before; he'd seen people die in movies many times—but could he really commit such an act? Let John come and find him, if he dared, but right now, it was best that he get as far away from that monster as he could.

The night crept in even faster than Jake had anticipated. Everything turned to grey and he could scarcely make out the houses. The street lights only seemed to emphasize the dark, rather than combat it. As he walked the laughter moved further into the distance and for a moment, Jake considered turning back, but even the shadowed streets were safer than home to him.

He stopped when he reached a street corner he didn't recognize. The sign read: *October Lane*. A wispy fog filled the street and made it hard to see anything beyond, but Jake felt compelled to explore this new part of the neighbourhood.

"Anything's better than going home," he said to himself before moving into the fog.

October Lane was a long, straight road flanked by rows of leafless, spindly trees. A full moon struggled to emerge through an ever-shifting veil of cloud, but there was just enough light to reveal the facades of some of the houses around him. Every yard was decorated for Halloween with gravestones, coffins, and spiderwebs. Some of the houses looked familiar, like Jake had seen them before on TV. One thing they all had in common was that they were devoid of trick-or-treaters of any kind.

A low growl stopped Jake dead in his tracks. Amongst the

tombstones he glimpsed the silhouette of a large dog peering at him with iridescent eyes. The sight of it sent a chill down into his gut and deeper into his bladder. The boy could suddenly hear every beat of his little heart.

"Should you be out walking these streets alone, child?"

Jake gasped as the tall man solidified out of the fog beside him. Swathed in a black robe, he towered over Jake. The boy could discern little from the man's face, apart from his captivating pale eyes. Jake took a step back, the nauseating sense of fear resting in his throat.

"Uh...hi..." was all Jake could manage.

*The man's obviously out for Halloween*, Jake told himself.

"Hello young man. What is your name?"

The lessons his mother had drummed into him about stranger danger kicked in. He took another few steps back and almost tripped on the kerb. The man slid around him and Jake realized he was surrounded by tombstones, cold stone grave markers, not foam, or cardboard, but actual stone.

"Your parents are not escorting you?" the man asked. His smile was the color of a fading bruise.

Jake looked for escape amongst the tombstones. "Leave me alone or...or I'll call for help!"

The man smiled wider, revealing pointed teeth. *They had to be fake fangs*, Jake thought. *They had to be.*

"Oh, please do scream, child... please do."

Jake broke into a run, brushing past the man. He felt the weave of his robes, but nothing else, almost as if the man wasn't there. Jake reached the road and followed the dividing line. In the thickening fog he couldn't get his bearings. He saw house after house, each more decrepit than the last. The surrounding trees were claws lashing at his shadow. In one window Jake saw a large floating eye, its iris flaring with malice.

"Help!" Jake said to the empty street.

He looked over his shoulder; he couldn't see the stranger, but that didn't mean he wasn't following. Jake turned about and ran back the way he thought he'd come. His hot breath mingled with the fog. The miasma was a thick wall of grey, all-encompassing.

The houses and trees had been swallowed by it.

"Help me please!" he cried to no one.

Then the fog split, as if two invisible hands were parting a curtain. Beyond, Jake beheld a wide cornfield with thousands of withered plants and, at its center, a scarecrow crucified. Jake thought his heart was going to stop. The scarecrow craned its hessian neck, the pointed hat atop its head drooping like a broken limb.

"I can help you Jake..." it said, before breaking into cackling laughter.

The corn plants began to rustle wildly as something within the crop came to life. The plants bent as the unseen thing came closer and closer. The boy screamed. He turned and ran again, but the street was eternal, the houses returned in never-ending rows. Jake felt tears on his face; he wanted his mother so much. He never should have left her.

"Mom! Please help me!"

Then the fog faded again and before him stood Shelley. He could hardly believe it.

"Mom! Mom! I'm here!"

The thinned cloud only provided a tantalising glimpse, like Jake was looking through tinted glass. He could see Shelley standing on the street corner—back in the real world. She was sobbing for her son while the trick-or-treating children laughed and cooed with joy, completely oblivious to her plight. None of them knew what lurked on the other side of Halloween.

"Mom!" Jake said.

His mother blinked away tears. Her lips were cracked and bloody with John's latest beating. There were finger-shaped bruises around her throat.

"I'm sorry, Jake," she said, her eyes not seeing her son standing in front of her.

Jake reached for her, but the fog was a burning shroud of ice. He recoiled in pain. "Mom! See me—please!"

"I'm sorry that I wasn't strong enough," she said. "I'm sorry that I wasn't a good enough mother...to you and Billy."

Jake wanted to tear down the fog wall, to take his mother's

hand. "No, Mom, I'm here! Why can't you see me!?"

Before his eyes Shelley began to fade, as if the fog was consuming her, as if she had never been there at all. Jake stared bewildered and terrified that everything he knew and loved was being wrenched away. Even through the fog he could still make out the movement of the happy children, but his mother was gone.

"Mom? Where did you go?" he said.

On the other side, another person stepped onto the corner—John. He stood tall, his whole body seething with anger and exertion. John scanned the street with sharp turns of his head—Jake wondered was he looking for Shelley, or was he looking for him? Jake backed away from the fog, still confused about where his mother had gone and praying that John couldn't see him.

"Where the hell are you, you little shit?" John said to himself.

Jake saw the tension in John's muscles, noticed the scratches on his cheek. There was fear in his eyes, and Jake knew something had happened. Something terrible.

"You better not come home, boy..." John said through gritted teeth.

Jake remembered the sorrow in his mother's voice before she'd faded away and the marks on her throat. John had done something to her.

John spoke again, but his voice was like the growl of some rabid dog. "...because if you do, you'll end up just like your good-for-nothing mother."

"No!" Jake screamed at the wall of fog. "No, you bastard!"

John, oblivious to Jake's presence, and preoccupied with the ramifications of his sin, turned his back on the boy and the street corner for good. The man just walked away. The fog closed in and plunged Jake's heart into darkness. He was trapped between monsters.

"You should never find yourself alone in this place, child."

Jake, realizing the horrible truth of his mother's fate, whirled about and lost his footing, toppling to the gritty asphalt.

The vampire, the scarecrow, the all-seeing eye and the black wolf loomed in, ravenous and impatient. They were going to devour Jake, soul and all. The boy closed his eyes, waiting for the killing strike: the sting of fangs, the rending of flesh. He was ready for it.

All he felt was the cruel touch of a cold night.

He opened his eyes and saw his would-be attackers had turned their backs on him. The lidless eye floated up the street, while the wolf slinked back between the tombstones. Only the vampire remained. The creature peered down upon him, not with hunger, but rather pity.

"You've found yourself lost in this place now, child," the vampire said.

Jake saw the others fade into nothing. They'd taken away his desire to die. Why? The vampire started to turn away, exuding only indifference.

"Why?" Jake said, urging the vampire to turn back. "Why won't you kill me?"

The vampire laughed, its body jerking beneath its cloak. "Oh, child," it said. "You were lost the moment you set foot on this very street."

A twinge of fear crept in, but Jake forced himself to his feet. "I wasn't lost—you lured me in here!"

The vampire shook his head and offered Jake his back once more. His voice trailed off, into the fog.

"You are lost, child…just like the rest of us. There's nothing here but loneliness, guilt and eternity."

Jake stood alone in the center of October Lane. His fear morphed into emptiness, like all his veins had been opened. He was hollow and hopelessly worthless. He would have cried…if he'd had even tears to shed.

He'd lost his mother…his future…and his soul…

All on October Lane.

# SECOND COMING CIRCUS

Father Coleman is saying the Lord's Prayer before bed when he starts coughing up blood.

The blood splatters across his bedsheets, scarlet against the white, and for the first time in his sixty-four years, he believes God is calling to him.

Pressing a hand to his lips to staunch the flow, Father Coleman gets to his knees and runs to the bathroom. He spits fresh blood into the sink and watches it slip down the drain. Thoughts race through his head and he studies himself in the mirror, sees the fear in his deep-set eyes. One thought, above all others, passes from his lips.

"Am I dying?"

A knock on the front door draws his gaze. *Who on earth is knocking on my door in the middle of the night?* He considers the blood, turns on the tap to rinse it away, and wipes his mouth on the back of his hand.

*Am I dying?*

*Who's at the door?*

The priest stands still, focuses on his breathing and pounding heart. The knock comes again. He checks his watch, and notices his hand is trembling. It's almost 1am. He has to hold mass in the morning.

*Why am I coughing up blood?*

The knock comes a third time. Father Coleman leaves the bathroom and steps into the hallway. Slowly, he shuffles along the carpet into the living room. Through the curtains, he glimpses two silhouettes standing at his front door. One of them reaches up to rap on the door.

*Knock-knock-knock*

*Whoever they are, they are persistent. Patient.*

"Who's there?" Father Coleman says, stifling a new cough.

The silhouettes turn in the direction of his voice.

"Servants of the Lord," one of them says.

The priest steps closer, leaning on his favorite recliner.

*Jehovah's Witness—at this hour?*

"Please," he says. "It's late—"

"Matthew Chapter 24, Verse 44: Therefore, you must also be ready, for the Son of Man is coming at an hour you do not expect… Padre."

The priest frowns and crosses to open the door. "How did you know I was a priest—"

The sight of the two men leaves Father Coleman speechless. One is horribly scarred, his face, neck and arms reddened and undulated with healed-over burns. The other, a tall, frail man glares back at him with sightless eyes the color of curdled milk. Despite their appearance, they each wear white shirts with black neckties and matching trousers.

"Your very door declares it so," the burned one says, indicating the crucifix nailed to the door frame.

Father Coleman forces a smile and a nod. "Yes, of course. Given that, do you think a Catholic priest truly requires a visit from the Jehovah's Witness?"

The burned one smiles back, revealing ridges in his lips. "The Lord always comes to his children in their hour of need."

The priest again nods in acknowledgement. "Indeed. Gentlemen, please don't take this the wrong way, but I am not feeling well and I have to hold mass in the morning. I do admire your dedication, but perhaps your mission would be better serving someone else who truly needs it?"

The burned Mormon holds his smile, while his partner continues to stand, unblinking.

"Are you troubled, Padre?"

"I beg your pardon?"

The burned one gestures to his blind companion. "Zachariah and I can sense that you are troubled—that you are holding some doubt in your heart. Not unlike the apostle Thomas, no?"

Coleman sighs and begins to close his door. "Forgive me, but as I said, I am unwell, not troubled. Goodnight, gentlemen."

The Mormon's voice trails in as the door closes. "Goodnight, Padre, may the Lord bless you and keep you."

He watches them leave down the street. Surely they won't bother anyone else in the middle of the night? He locks the door, walks to the bathroom to rinse out his mouth, prays that the blood is an anomaly, changes his sheets, and suddenly weary, falls asleep.

Glass shatters, rousing Father Coleman from his slumber.

He sits up in bed, listening intently to the dark. He knows he heard the sound of something breaking. Through the echoes of the wind and the steady trill of the cicadas, his ears focus on the tinkling of glass.

He pulls the blankets closer, the beat of his heart and the taste of blood throbbing in the back of his throat. Again, the fear comes, even sharper than before.

*Am I going to die?*

The cicadas cease their song and the silence takes hold. Coleman considers calling out, and estimates the distance between his bedroom and the phone in the living room. The glass. The glass will be everywhere. All over the floor. He'll cut his feet. There'll be so much blood.

*This is my blood.*

He peers at the rectangle of darkness that separates his bedroom from the hall. It's like a freshly dug grave.

"Who's there?" he says to the grave.

The blind Mormon bleeds out of the black, a ghost from the void. Despite his frailty and blindness, Zachariah seems to know exactly where Father Coleman is.

The priest screams and tastes his blood all over again.

Father Coleman awakes to a cacophony of sobbing and fear. He blinks against the dim light, silhouettes of people emerging through the fog in his head. The faces of the people seated around him sharpen with each breath and he sees that each of them is just as terror-stricken as he is. He tries to stand, but quickly realizes he is bound to his chair, the others too. There are four others: a woman, possibly in her early thirties, and three men of varying ages. One of the men bears a bloody gash above his eye. All of them struggle against their bonds. The priest, discomforted by their desperate appearances, looks away to the walls.

*Where am I?*

*Who are these people?*

The walls, grimy and flecked with dirt, are adorned floor to ceiling with bands of red and white. The more Coleman examines the walls, the more he believes them to be moving, shifting as if in a gentle breeze. Head swimming, he cranes his neck to look upwards to discover the ceiling reaches a pointed apex above them.

"It's a tent," Coleman whispers. "I'm in a tent."

"Please…"

He turns to the woman's voice. Her mascara runs like black snakes down her cheeks.

"Mister, please…can you help me get loose?"

Coleman pulls against the ropes, his skin stinging in resistance. "How did I get here?" he replies. "How did you?"

One of the men—the one with the gash over his eye—speaks up, the timbre of his voice wavering.

"Shut the fuck up! They'll hear. They'll come back."

A rising bellow of music startles them—the warbling thunder of a pipe organ. The interior of the tent swells with impossible light from an invisible source and it is then that Coleman understands just how spacious the tent is. He and the others are seated around a stage and towering above it is the gargantuan pipe organ.

"Oh, God! Oh, Jesus!" the bleeding man cries.

The organ music soars inside Coleman's ears, a rising throng that none of them can block. It flows around them and through them, and yet the shadows keep the organist a mystery. The priest just wants the song to stop and as if by his command, it does.

Two figures enter the stage like they are made of the air itself. Zachariah and his burned companion. Sweat runs down Coleman's back as they approach, clutching black, leatherbound books. The priest's fellow hostages begin to keen and moan in despair.

"Please..." the woman says. "Don't hurt me."

The burned Mormon—if he truly is a Christian at all—holds out his hands to try to soothe his captive audience.

"Oh, Miss Chisholm, we're not going to hurt you—we're going to enlighten you." He turns to Father Coleman. "We have a newcomer to our flock—an actual man of the cloth."

Coleman swallows down his fear. "Why have you brought me here? You need to let me go." He looks to the others. "You need to let us all go."

He ignores the priest. "Father Coleman here believes he knows God. He's been the dutiful servant, holding mass, celebrating feast days, fasting during Lent, breaking the bread, and blessing the communion wine. For years, he has believed that God was speaking to him—through him. But he is wrong."

He moves from the priest to Miss Chisholm, who recoils in her chair. "Sally Chisholm once walked God's path, but in her weakness, she strayed, choosing illicit substances and fornication. She refused to hear God's word, she used her mouth to please men instead of speaking the Lord's gospel, and her eyes?" He reaches out to touch her cheek, but she wrenches her face away. "...Through her eyes, she saw only sin."

Zachariah descends the stairs and places a book in each of the hostage's laps. Still, he walks and moves as if he can see. Coleman looks down and sees the book is a collection of hymns. The burned man continues.

"I, Jacob, have brought you here to summon you to His fold. To show you that God has returned to this world to bring forth his judgement as the one true redeemer."

The pipe organ starts anew, filling the air with its melancholy. Zachariah opens the hymnals for each of them, but Coleman realizes the pages are blank. Jacob and Zachariah begin to sing.

"The blood of the Lamb
Is a river to cleanse the sinner..."

The organ reaches a crescendo of sound and Coleman's ears—all of their ears—ring in pain. Sally Chisholm screams, her hearing seemingly the worst affected. Coleman watches in horror as blood oozes from her ear canals, dripping down the sides of her face. Still the organ plays its vile tune and still Jacob and Zachariah sing.

"Our Lord, our Lamb has come
To save the righteous.
His blood, our blood,
Is water for the soul."

More parishioners appear on the stage from the dark, clothed in matching white and black. Each of them carries some nature of deformity: a missing arm or leg, burns and cuts. Others have their mouths and eyes stitched closed. They begin to sway in time with the music, joining in the chorus. Sally Chisholm writhes in agony beside the priest.

"The blood of the Lamb
Is a river to cleanse
The sinner.
We feel his love through
Silence, patience, and grace.
His blood, our blood,
Is water for the soul."

The man with the gash above his eye pries his hands free and tries to run, but Zachariah grabs him by his hair and forces him to the ground. The organ ceases its song and the gathered flock moves down to circle the melee.

"Get the fuck off me!" the man says, trying to escape the blind man's grip.

"Silence him, Zachariah," Jacob says, "Silence him so he can hear His word."

One of them produces a hooked needle, another a thread of catgut. Each is handed to Zachariah. The gashed man struggles, but the flock holds his limbs tight. Those same greedy fingers keep his head pinned down as the needle pierces his upper lip. The man's screams echo off the revival tent walls and the organ restarts in celebration. Coleman grimaces as Zachariah meticulously weaves the hook and thread through the man's lips, sealing them closed.

"His blood, our blood
Is water for the soul."

Sally stops screaming. "I…I can hear him," she says.

Coleman and the other victims turn to her, watching as her expression shifts from confusion to elation.

"I can hear him!"

Jacob goes to her, joyous. "Of course you can! You only needed to listen. We all only need to listen."

The second man pisses his pants, the sound of the torrent drawing their gazes. Jacob tuts in disappointment.

"Gerry here is a slave to his fear. Help him see that there is nothing to fear."

The group moves without hesitation. Coleman sits unblinking as they draw back the man's head, while two others go at his eyes with pocket knives. After the screams fade, they present Jacob with two red orbs. For a moment, he holds them in his palm like they are jewels, only to drop them to the floor and squash them beneath his heel.

"Now Gerry will see His wonders."

Father Coleman straightens is his chair, trying to remain steadfast against the ensuing madness.

"What you are doing is not God's work," the priest says to Jacob.

The others look to the priest, their work leaving Gerry with two red caverns in his skull, but subdued and reverent.

"These sinners have seen the light, Father," Jacob says. "Gerry has seen it…" He then points to the other man with the sewn lips. "Brian there has heard it, as has Sally. The only one left to understand the truth is you."

Coleman coughs. "Do you think this is what God meant when He wanted you to spread His word? Blinding and maiming people?"

Jacob shrugs. "The Lord works in mysterious ways."

Coleman scoffs, but it starts a coughing fit. He spits bloody phlegm on the floor. Jacob observes the blood puddle and then steps closer to the old priest.

"Death is what you fear, isn't it, Padre?"

"No, because I believe in the resurrection."

The leader smiles. "You don't need to be resurrected, Father. God gave us these bodies—this flesh—to be His temple, His church here on Earth. He never wanted us to build places of stone and wood to worship Him in. Our blood is His soul.

The group recites Jacob's words in turn.

*"Our blood is His soul. His soul is our blood."*

Gerry, blood oozing from his eye sockets, joins them. "His soul is in our blood."

Sally is untied and she walks over to join the flock. "His soul is in our blood," she says.

Jacob dips a finger in Father Coleman's blood and shows it to him. "His blood is in your blood too, Padre."

"No," the priest says.

"You proclaim it to be His blood at communion. Why is it so hard for you to believe it resides in each of us?"

Coleman looks into Jacob's eyes and each of the others in turn. They are afflicted with a shared madness. Then the leader takes the priest's hands in his.

"Oh, Padre, everything is a shared madness."

"What? How did you—

Jacob stands and summons the flock to his side. "Shall we show him?"

They converge on him, scooping him up, chair and all, to carry him to the stage.

"No, please—don't!" the priest says.

"But Padre, you said it yourself—you don't fear death because of the resurrection!"

He is carried across the stage, the organ stirring them all in their procession. At the end of the stage, a glowing crack of light begins to appear. A thin line of golden light. The doors to the tent are parting.

"He is already resurrected, Father," Jacob says. "He came to me as a boy on my parents' farm. They wanted to destroy Him. They saw Him as an aberration, but I knew what He was. He was a gift, like the Son he sent to us two thousand years ago."

The tent doors part wide and beyond them Father Coleman beholds a lamb seated atop a field of lush grass. The lamb is eyeless, its mouth sealed over with skin, unformed. Seven legs, instead of four. Its wool gleams with ethereal light and the priest can hear its voice—its soul—in his head.

The priest feels the warmth of its light and for the second time in his life, he understands that God is calling him.

# OCTOBERVILLE

The highway was a never-ending black vein winding through the night.

The headlights of Tom Crane's rental car barely illuminated the road, or the thick forest that loomed on either side. Tom wanted to be anywhere but the road; most of all he wanted to be home, with Sally and Tom Jr. His job as marketing manager had become so demanding over the last six months that it had taken on a life of its own and he feared it was the only life he was ever going to have.

Tom stared out the window at the forest blurring by. Black ash trees, tall and spindly, disappeared into the last remnants of twilight, lost to the impending dark. Tom was starting to feel lost within that darkness when his cell phone rang. Seeing it was Sally, he pressed the receiver button on the steering wheel to answer.

"Hey babe," he said, trying hard not to let his weariness come across over the phone.

"Hey, how are you—where are you?" Sally said.

Tom recalled the last signpost he'd seen. "Uh, about 10 miles outside Hayward, I think."

"You're still in Wisconsin? Tom, it's almost seven pm—I thought you'd be closer to home."

Tom sighed at the exasperation in Sally's voice. "Hey, look, I'm sorry, honey. The conference went over time. Dale needed to talk to me after."

"Weren't you supposed to leave early this morning? It's

Halloween and Tom Jr.'s expecting you. I don't know why Dale just didn't fly you down like usual."

Tom squeezed the steering wheel. "I know, I know. I'm sorry. The conference just took a whole different direction once Dale brought out the annual sales report."

"Was it bad?"

Tom rubbed an eye with the palm of his hand. "Yeah, it was bad—and that's why I'm driving home, instead of flying. The sales figures were bad and Dale was just looking at me the entire time he spoke. Then, when he pulled me aside after, he grilled me about my plans for the new campaign. He was really stressed out, which only stressed me out."

"Are you saying he thinks it's your fault sales are down?"

"Well, I am the marketing manager, honey."

"Hey, there's no need to take it out on me, Tom."

Tom looked back to the forest, as if it contained the answer to all his problems. He took some deep, calming breaths. Something shifted between the trees in his field of vision, the shape keeping pace with his car. When he blinked, it was gone.

"Look, honey, I can't tell you how sorry I am," Tom said, as he tried to both watch the road and see where the shape was. "I've just had a really long day. I don't think I'm going to make it back in time to take Tommy trick-or-treating."

Sally sighed. "He's going to be so disappointed."

"I know and I'm sorry—"

The shape rushed out from the woods right in front of Tom's car. He swore and jerked the wheel to try and avoid a collision. The car skidded and bounced off the road into the line of trees. He slammed his foot on the brake, but the car slid across the carpet of fallen leaves like it was ice. He screamed his wife's name as the trunk of an enormous Ash tree came into view.

Seconds later, a sea of darkness swallowed Tom whole.

When Tom came to on the side of the road he opened his eyes to behold a solitary word.

OCTOBERVILLE.

His whole body ached, but when he moved, his skull felt like it was going to explode. Gingerly, he touched his forehead and his fingers came away slick with blood. He rolled onto his side and saw his car across the road, crumpled around the Ash tree. Through the ache in his head, he tried to figure out if he'd been thrown from the wreckage, or whether he'd managed to climb out. He couldn't recall any details after crashing into the tree. Very gently, he turned his head to look back to the spot where he'd seen the word.

The road sign read:

OCTOBERVILLE—2 MILES.

Slowly he pulled himself to his knees, then stood. The highway swayed beneath his feet for a moment, but after he took a few slow, deep breaths, the world became straight and steady. Apart from the ache in his head, he didn't seem to have suffered any other injuries. He questioned whether he was capable of walking two miles to the town, but told himself he should call an ambulance instead. He started to cross the street to grab his cell from its cradle in the car, when the wreck burst into flames with a *WHOOMPF!* The sight mesmerized him for several moments until the inevitability of it sank in. He was hurt, stranded and alone. All that was left to do was to walk into the night towards Octoberville.

The throb in Tom's head lessened with each step, for which he was grateful. The flap of a bird taking flight from a tree to his left startled him and the image of the beast-like shape rushing out from the woods in front of his car slapped his subconscious. He rubbed his weary eyes, trying to make sense of what he thought he'd seen. There hadn't been any beast; he'd just been tired, and distracted by the hypnotic nature of the road and the conversation with his wife. He thought of Sally and Tom Jr. and sadness pricked at his eyes. The last thing Sally would have heard was him screaming her name; maybe she would try and send someone to find him? Or maybe she never heard him at all? Maybe the phone reception cut out and they had no idea what had happened, or where he was? After all, Sally didn't expect him home for hours. At that moment his wife and son were likely walking the neighborhood, trick-or-treating. Tom imagined his son dressed up in the zombie outfit they'd made together. His tears flowed.

The highway curved to the right and as Tom shuffled along, a thin layer of fog drifted out from a cleared space in the woods. A rusted gate creaked gently in the evening breeze. Tom squinted through the fog and saw the unmistakable silhouettes of tombstones. Beams of moonlight sliced through the wispy miasma like shards of glass. As he tried to understand why a cemetery would be so close to the highway, he heard the sharp, rhythmic chop of steel striking earth. The sound drew Tom closer, and a much taller silhouette appeared. Someone was digging.

"Hello?" Tom called.

The shadow stopped digging and walked towards him.

"Who's that?"

The man emerged into the moonlight. He removed his cap and revealed a grizzled, old face.

"Please, sir, you have to help me," Tom said, and almost ran to the old man. "There was an accident. I've been injured."

The old man rubbed his grey beard and lifted his shovel, as if arming himself.

"You came from the highway?" the old man said.

"Yes! Yes, my car hit a tree."

The old man looked him up and down, taking notice of the blood on Tom's face. "I see. You'll be wanting to go into town then, I suppose?"

"Please. I need to call my wife and son and let them know what happened."

The old man poked a thumb over his shoulder. "I was just finishing up filling in a grave. You caught me just in time. I can take you into town. The name's Vernon."

"I'm so glad I found you, Vernon. My name's Tom. So, you can take me to… Octoberville?"

"That's right. Come on, my truck's this way."

Tom had never been so happy to see another human being. Thankfully the truck was a short walk. It was a rust-flecked, beaten-up old thing. The doors and vinyl seats squeaked loudly when they climbed inside. On the dash, Tom noticed a long length of sharpened wood and a clove of garlic hanging from the rear-view mirror. A chrome-plated revolver sat in the center of the seat. Tom frowned at all the items and the old man as he started the truck, which roared like some sort of monster. Vernon gave him a nod and a wink.

"Next stop, Octoberville."

Ironically, Octoberville was just around the bend, not even half a mile. As they drove towards it, Tom noticed the roadside was marked with carved pumpkins, all gleaming with candlelight, like a queer landing strip.

"I've never seen Halloween decorations on a highway before."

Vernon gave him a sideways glance. "Huh, wait until you see the town. It is called Octoberville."

"So, was it settled in October or something?"

"You could say that."

Tom watched the garlic swinging, almost hypnotically. He wanted to ask Vernon about the sharpened stick and the gun, but thought better of it. Ahead, Tom made out the shape of a tall spire atop a hall in the town square. He wrung his hands, eager to get to a telephone and call his family. Some people were walking along the side of the road towards town. Adults with excited children dressed in their Halloween costumes. Tom thought of his son. When he put his head out the window as they drove past to get a look at one boy he gasped. Both the father and son's faces were covered with scales, like a snake. He quickly ducked back inside, a pang of uneasiness building in his gut.

"Everything okay there, Tom?" Vernon asked.

"Uh…yeah. You folks sure do get into Halloween."

Vernon chuckled. "It's our favorite holiday. And here we are."

The old man turned into the main road of the town. A great sign, immaculately carved from a single piece of wood in the shape of a pumpkin, and still retaining its clean, hand-painted luster, read: WELCOME TO OCTOBERVILLE, POP: 10,031.

There were trick-or-treaters everywhere: children and adults in full costume, vampires, mummies, aliens, devils with pitchforks, and sea monsters, all laughing and running in the streets, giving each other candy. For some reason, the sight made Tom's heart pound. A line of dead-looking oak trees dominated the street and hundreds of orange lights dangled between them on clumpy lines of cobweb. Adults wore painted monster faces, while some children wore monster masks. Elsewhere, a group of men in queer robes led a procession, handing out treats and cakes to the children. Tom saw one child bite into a cake to find a large eyeball inside. The child swallowed it whole. Tom was amazed at how realistic the candy and costumes all looked. The truck pulled up on the side of the road and at first, Tom was afraid to get out.

"I'll take you up to the sheriff's office and you can phone from there," Vernon told Tom.

Tom climbed out of the truck and everyone stopped to stare at him. Werewolf children, with their witch mothers and fanged fathers.

"Well, who's that you got there, Vernon?"

A rotund man, dressed as a zombie, complete with exposed intestines, stepped up to them. Tom took a step back when he got a look at the man's shredded form.

"Well, hey there Mayor Kirkman. This here is Tom. I found him on the highway just past the cemetery. He had himself an accident."

The Mayor's torn lips drooped. "Well, ain't that a crying shame."

Tom scanned all the Halloween revelers. "I…uh, was hoping to use a phone, to call home. My wife and son will be wondering where I am."

Mayor Kirkman smiled, but his bottom lip still hung low. Tom thought his makeup was astounding. "Of course, of course," he said. "I'll take you up to see the sheriff."

"Uh…thank you."

The Mayor addressed the crowd. "Okay everyone, back to it now."

The crowd dispersed; the laughter and frivolity coming back on like a switch. The zombified Mayor put a decrepit arm around Tom's shoulder and led him into town. Tom didn't know where to look; he'd never seen so much Halloween in all his life, particularly amongst adults.

"So, Tom, you had an accident you say?" the Mayor asked.

"Yeah, I was driving back home from a conference and this… animal ran out in front of my car. I tried to swerve to avoid hitting it and ended up colliding with a tree."

"Oh, I'm very sorry to hear that, Tom. I see you've taken a knock on the head. We might have to get our town doctor to take a look at you."

"If it's not too much trouble."

Mayor Kirkman patted Tom on the back. "No trouble at all," he said. "Here's the sheriff's office. I'll introduce you, but then I'll have to get straight back into the festivities."

"You sure do get into the spirit of the holiday."

Kirkman smiled that ghoulish smile. "Every day is Halloween in Octoberville, Tom."

They opened the door to the sheriff's office and Tom saw a man seated at a desk, dressed in a black and white puritan costume, complete with a tall hat. Even the law seemed to be obsessed with Halloween.

"Ah, Sheriff Price, we've got a newcomer," Mayor Kirkman said. "He says he had an accident on the road, just past the cemetery. Old Vernon found him."

The sheriff stood and Tom was taken aback by how tall and imposing he was. "Truly?" the sheriff said.

"Ah, where are my manners?" the mayor said. "Tom, this is Sheriff Price. I'll leave you in his very capable hands. Sheriff, I'll see you later at the cauldron."

The sheriff nodded and the mayor shambled out the door, getting back into character. Tom swallowed hard as Octoberville's obsession started to get the better of him.

"Why don't you sit down, Tom?" Sheriff Price said. "You must be exhausted."

"Uh, thanks. Yes, I am a bit." Tom sat and saw the old turn-dial telephone on the desk. "I was really hoping to call my family. Let them know what's happened."

The sheriff opened a large leather book and dipped a quill pen in a jar of ink. "All in good time; right now, I need to record your accident."

"Please, Sheriff, I just need to call home."

The sheriff kept writing in large cursive letters. "What is your surname?"

"Uh, Crane."

"And what is your profession?"

"I'm…I'm a marketing manager for a sales company."

"What does your company sell?"

"Knife sets."

The sheriff raised an eyebrow. "Interesting… So tell me how you crashed your vehicle?"

"An animal ran out in front of me and I swerved to miss it and ended up crashing into a tree."

The sheriff looked at Tom, his eyes narrowed. "An animal?"

"Yes."

"What did it look like?"

Tom's headache returned, the throb beating in time with his frantic heart. "I don't know. It happened so fast. Please, I just need to call home."

The Sheriff reached for the telephone. "I'll call Dr. Steiner so he can check on you."

Tom watched the sheriff dial. "I want to call my wife."

The sheriff ignored him. "Dr. Steiner, this is Sheriff Price. If you could come down to my office, we've got a walk-in who might have a concussion." He put down the phone and considered Tom again, his pale gaze more scrutinizing.

"The animal—exactly how tall was it?"

"How tall? Uh… Look I really don't know what to tell you."

"Mr. Crane, it might be very important."

Tom shrugged and fidgeted; the sheriff's questions and tone were becoming invasive. "I'm sorry, that's all I can tell you."

The door opened and a bespectacled man in a white lab coat entered. He carried a large, black leather medical bag. He looked too young and unkempt to be a doctor, Tom thought.

"Well, well, who do we have here?" the doctor said with a high-pitched, grating timbre.

"This is Mr. Tom Crane," the sheriff said. "He was in a car accident and bumped his head.

The doctor bent in close and Tom could see wildness in his eyes. "Bumped his head, eh? Perhaps some injury to the brain?" He leaned to touch at Tom's head wound, and Tom flinched.

"He also may have seen the beast," the sheriff added, and this piqued the doctor's interest.

"The beast-man?" he said, before looking to Tom. "You saw the beast-man?"

Tom scrambled to his feet and backed away. "What the hell is wrong with you people? I think you're taking Halloween a little too seriously."

The sheriff stood and folded his arms behind his back. "Please take a seat Mr. Crane, so Dr. Steiner can examine you."

Dr. Steiner sneered and tittered. His eyes were wide and ogling. "Yes, come on Mr. Crane, let Dr. Steiner take a good look at you."

"No, no thank you." The two men stepped closer, as if they knew he intended to run. "I think I'll just make my way back to the highway.

"The highway isn't safe," Steiner said. "The beast-man is always hungry on Halloween!"

Tom turned and ran for the door. He burst out into the street and met a wall of people. The entire town must have been standing outside the sheriff's office, waiting, watching and listening. All their macabre faces locked on his.

"Get back!" Tom said. "All of you get back!"

"Tom, come now, I think you need to calm down."

It was Mayor Kirkman; he dragged himself through the crowd towards him. He tried to give Tom a comforting smile, but his face seemed so rotten.

"Stay away from me!"

The mayor held out his peeling hands. "Tom it's okay. Everyone finds Octoberville strange at first, but you'll get used to it."

Tom ran. He knocked over a man who looked like Frankenstein's monster, but the crowd didn't retaliate. They simply parted and let him through. As he ran down the street towards the road that led to the highway, he heard Mayor Kirkman tell Vernon to go after him. Tom's head pounded with each step, with each breath, but he had to keep going. The people of Octoberville were insane. He imagined that if they caught him they would sacrifice him to the devil or some great jack-o'-lantern.

Legs aching, Tom glanced over his shoulder to make sure no one was coming and thankfully, there was nobody in sight. He reached the highway and ran in the direction he'd come. He knew Hayward was at least fifteen miles away, but he hoped a car would stop and help him.

He ran for what seemed like forever. The glowing pumpkins either side of the road appeared to laugh at his misfortune. Just when he began to tire, the cemetery came into view, spurring him on. He had to get as far away from Octoberville, from the Halloween madness.

A guttural growl had him whirl on his feet. Behind him, less than six feet away, stood what had to be the beast-man. In the light of the full moon, Tom saw that its face, hands and feet were covered in fur, but it wore a button-up shirt and trousers. Drool slipped from its large fangs, and Tom screamed.

"No! No! Don't scream, please!" the beast-man said. It held up its paws to placate him.

Tom thought his heart was going to stop.

"Please, don't scream," the beast-man said. "I don't like it when they scream."

"Don't...don't eat me," Tom said, but the words trailed off. The beast-man became a blur once more, as did everything around him.

And the darkness swallowed Tom a second time.

Tom awoke in a bright white room on top of an examination bed. He sat up and stared at the medical charts on the walls, the shelves of medical utensils, the jars of tissue samples suspended in bile-colored liquid. He realized he must have been in Steiner's office, that the beast-man had brought him back to Octoberville to be cut up like some lab rat. Tom jumped off the bed and went to open the door and escape when it opened of its own accord.

Dr. Steiner, the sheriff, Mayor Kirkman and even Vernon entered the room. Following close behind was the beast-man and another even taller man in a white theatrical mask and black overalls. Tom backed away, but there was nowhere to go.

"You can't kill me!" Tom said.

"Mr. Crane, do calm down," Sheriff Price said.

"My family is probably already calling the police! They'll find my car!"

The mayor raised a hand to try and quiet him. "Tom, we've already collected what was left of your car and brought it back here."

Steiner smiled. "You're stuck here, I'm afraid."

The masked man held up a set of knives. The wood was scorched, but the steel was still brand new. He pulled the largest one free and Tom recoiled.

"Kenneth here found your car and this set of knives in the trunk," Vernon said. "He loves a good knife, he does."

"Please! Look, if you let me go, I won't tell anyone about this place!" Tom said.

The beast-man stepped closer. It seemed unable to look him in the eye, as if bashful. "I'm sorry Mr. Crane, about what I did. I didn't mean to."

Tom tried to catch his breath as the six figures closed in. "Wha-what?"

"When I jumped in front of your car," the beast-man said, his yellow eyes now on his hairy feet. "I didn't mean to spook you."

"It…it was you?"

Vernon came forward then, the seemingly kind old gravedigger. He took off his hat. "You see, Ralph wanders a bit at night and usually finds himself in some trouble or another. But he's got a good temperament. He don't hurt nobody on purpose. He's trying to say that he's sorry he caused the accident that brought you here."

Tom looked from one to the other. He told himself he had to be dreaming, that this was a vivid nightmare about Halloween.

"What…are you talking about?"

"Tom," Mayor Kirkman said. "I'm afraid you're dead. When your car hit the tree, you died."

"I'm so sorry," Ralph the beast-man said, wiping a tear from his eye.

Tom swallowed down the urge to retch. "I… How…how can I be dead? I'm standing here."

"Yes, yes, you are," Dr. Steiner said. "But this is Octoberville."

None of them made sense. Nothing made sense. "No…"

"What's the last thing you remember, Mr. Crane?" the sheriff asked.

"Waking…waking up on the side of the road…"

"And seeing the sign to Octoberville, right?" the mayor said.

Tom could see the sign in his mind: OCTOBERVILLE—2 MILES.

The mayor placed a decaying hand on Tom's shoulder. "I'm sorry Tom, but this is where you end up when you die on Halloween."

It wasn't until Tom saw his own burned corpse inside the blackened car wreck that he truly believed he was dead.

"Don't worry," Vernon said. "I'll take good care of you; give you a proper burial like everyone else. We've all got a story like yours," Vernon said.

"We're all in the same boat," Dr. Steiner added, chuckling.

The mayor went to Tom's side and placed that reassuring arm around his shoulder. "But there is a bright side."

Tom felt it ironic that he could still cry. "How? How can there be a bright side to the fact that I'm dead?"

The mayor smiled and half his face opened up. "This is Octoberville!"

They took Tom outside and Halloween was still going on. The main street was overflowing with people—dead people who got to spend eternity celebrating summer's end. Tom knew he was a part of it now, but he wasn't ready to give up his past. The mayor escorted Tom through the crowds and now everyone in Octoberville offered him a smile.

"Before, when we were alive, we used to think that Halloween was about candy and costumes," he said. "And it is, but it's also much more than that. You know why?"

Tom shook his head and it only made the zombie mayor smile anew.

"Because it's also about doors opening."

The mayor pointed to the hall with its spire at the end of the street and Tom could see its doors were wide open. A blazing light poured out and through it, Tom could see Sally and Tom Jr., walking the neighborhood back home, trick-or-treating. Tom turned back to the mayor and gave him a smile of his own.

"Like I said, my friend," the mayor told him. "Every day is Halloween in Octoberville!"

# THE HISTORY OF HALLOWEEN

Lyla Martin stared at the Halloween decorations on the door to the recording studio at Radio 2NGB and realized how kitsch her life had become.

The fake cobwebs, plastic pumpkins, and the five-and-something-feet-tall skeleton framed the door like a wreath, but Lyla didn't think they'd scare even the smallest child. Halloween, sadly, was becoming a joke.

The deathly visage of the skeleton seemed to mock her, the red LED lights inside its eye sockets blinking in unison with the phrase swirling around her head:

FA-KER

FA-KER

FA-KER

Lyla turned to her cell phone and noticed her inbox was now pushing past one hundred emails. October 31st was her busiest day of the year, so busy she thought she needed an assistant to handle all the interview and presentation requests. After this interview with Radio 2NGB, she had to dash across town to the headquarters of the New Hampshire Historical Society to present a seminar on her upcoming book, *Halloween Histories*—a seemingly impossible task she was still in the process of writing.

But Lyla Martin had to give the people what they wanted—every possible detail on Halloween and why the world, particularly the United States, was still obsessed with the holiday.

Her phone pinged with a new email from Renata Dawson, Secretary of the New Hampshire Historical Society:

Happy Halloween Ms. Martin!

I am just writing to confirm your appearance at our hall, this morning. Everyone is just dying to hear about your next book!

Sincerely,
Renata

Lyla rolled her eyes and fired back a short reply of thanks. Renata was starting to push the boundaries of their professional relationship. After this seminar, Lyla thought it might be time to decline any future invitations. No amount of money would convince her to try and explain Halloween to a bunch of wannabe history buffs every year, ad infinitum.

The door to the recording booth opened and a tall, burly man with bushy grey hair and matching beard emerged. Radio 2NGB host, Tim Bryce. He offered her a strong handshake and a broad smile.

"Lyla, so great to see you again," he said.

Lyla smirked and nodded. "It's great to see you too, Tim."

He gestured to the door. "What do you think of our Halloween decorations? Our receptionist Sally put some real effort in this time."

Lyla looked the door up and down again. So, going down to the nearest Dollar Store and spending a few bucks on whatever was on the shelf was considered a *real effort* these days, Lyla thought to herself.

"Looks great!" Lyla said.

"Sally will be happy to hear that," Tim said. "Well, come on through to the booth. We'll be going live in a few minutes."

Lyla sat opposite Tim and put her handbag under the desk, ensuring her cell phone was on silent. The directional microphone seemed to reach out for her like a disembodied arm.

"We're going to open for questions at the end of our chat, if that's okay, Lyla?"

"Sure, that's no problem."

"Fantastic. Well, did you want Sally to fix you a coffee, or anything?"

Lyla popped on her headset. "No, I'm good. Ready to go whenever you are."

"Oh, champing at the bit, are we? That's fantastic. Okay, well, I'll just get started as soon as this song finishes."

Lyla hadn't paid much attention to the song being played over the speakers, but she wasn't surprised to hear it was *Monster Mash*. Tim played that song every Halloween.

"Monster Mash is such an iconic song, don't you think, Lyla?" he said with a Cheshire cat grin.

"It sure is."

Tim held up a finger as the song faded out and launched into his spiel.

"Hey, welcome back everyone! Well, it's time for our main event—the interview you've all been waiting for on this spooky Halloween morning. Our chat with Halloween expert, Lyla Martin. Welcome back to Radio 2NGB, Lyla!"

"Thanks for having me back, Tim."

Lyla sat perfectly still, picking anxiously at her fingernails under the desk as Tim continued his introduction.

"Lyla is a New Hampshire native, author, and historian. Her book, *Halloween Horrors,* made the US Today Bestseller list, but her biggest achievement in my opinion is that she was actually born on Halloween. Isn't that right, Lyla?"

Tim flashed her a smile and Lyla smirked back. "Um, yes, that's right, Tim."

"Lyla, have you ever considered that the reason you know so much about Halloween is because you were born on October $31^{st}$?"

Lyla cleared her throat nervously. "Oh, no, I think it's purely coincidence."

"Have you ever gone back into your family history or anything? Weren't any witches in your family, were there?"

Tim seemed to run with the same jokes every year as well.

"Not as far as I know, Tim, but in truth, I've never really looked into it."

Lyla gave Tim a slight glare, as if to say, *where are you going with this—stick to the script!* But he laughed, a guffaw that made him bounce like Santa Claus.

"Okay then, let's move along. So, let's dive into all things Halloween. Lyla, can you tell us how you became so invested in Halloween? How did you become such an expert—was it something you grew up with?"

Lyla cleared her throat again as she conjured a mental image of her parents repeatedly telling her she wasn't allowed to celebrate the holiday with her friends, how her father always used to pray over her at bedtime instead of reading her a story. She blinked the thoughts aside and answered.

"Well, actually, no, I didn't grow up with Halloween. In fact, we didn't celebrate at home at all."

Tim's eyes widened. "Wow, you've never mentioned that before, Lyla. So, it wasn't a thing in your home?"

"No. I was raised in a Christian home where Halloween was frowned upon as being something, well…evil. But the thing is, my curiosity about Halloween grew from that very denial. I secretly learned all I could about Halloween and once, I even snuck out to trick or treat."

Tim leaned closer to the microphone. Lyla didn't know why she was revealing so much of her past.

"Gee, I bet your parents weren't happy about that," he said.

"No, they weren't. When they found out, I was grounded for several weeks. But, in the end, it didn't stop me from fostering my passion for Halloween."

"What do your parents think of your chosen line of work these days?"

"My parents are both deceased."

"Oh, I'm very sorry to hear that."

Tim didn't know what to say so there was an awkward silence, which didn't suit live radio. He quickly adjusted himself.

"So, Lyla, what about the perception of um, evil around Halloween? I was always brought up to believe it was fun."

"Yes, it is meant to be fun. These days, particularly in the US, the holiday is all about trick-or-treating, yard haunts, and candy. But the connotation that Halloween is evil is a total misconception. Some connected Halloween to the Celtic festival, Samhain, which signifies the end of summer. It's celebrated on October 31st as the time to start preparing for winter and because the Celts saw it as a new year type festival, they believed it was also the time when the veil between the worlds was at its thinnest and that some spirits could cross over. But it's not associated with evil and the Celts did not worship a Lord of the Dead or make sacrifices. That's just something that organized religion locked onto and spread to try and discourage children from participating."

"I see." Tim checked the screen on the recording panel. "Well, apparently, we're already getting some questions. So, listeners, you can now call our hotline to ask Lyla some questions on 555-2NGB. That's 555-2642. Hello, you're on the air!"

A woman's excited voice came over the speaker. "Oh, hi! Hi! My name is Marie. Great to meet you, Tim! And Lyla!"

"Hi, Marie, do you have a question for Lyla?"

"Yes, yes. Um, Lyla, can you tell me why people started checking candy? Was it true that people tried to poison kids' candy because they were against Halloween?"

Lyla scoffed. "None of that happened. There were cases of people doing it, but they weren't these anonymous psychos. One woman, years ago, didn't like older kids trick-or-treating and would put ant buttons into their baskets and that was blown out of proportion with this idea that people were putting razor blades in candy. It's all just something that became an urban legend."

"Oh, okay," Marie said. "That's interesting. Thank you, Lyla!"

Tim nodded Lyla's way, but then he pressed his headset on tighter. "We have another caller on the line. Welcome to Radio 2NGB Breakfast. Who do we have on the line?"

Lyla listened intently as a strange silence pervaded the booth. But a sound did rise, like the echo of what sounded like a howling wind rushing through a tunnel.

"Hmm, looks like someone's calling from outside their home?" Tim said. "Hello? Is anyone there?"

The wind constricted, focusing to become one word: "Lyyylllaaaaaaaa!"

Lyla froze in her seat and shared a look of terror with Tim, whose face suddenly matched the tone of his beard.

"Okay, we don't appreciate prank calls here, even if it is Halloween—"

The voice boomed over Tim's:

LYYYYLLLLAAAAA'S SSSOOOULLLLLL!"

Feedback burst in their ears, like an electric guitar held too close to a speaker. Lyla and Tim wrenched their headsets away before Tim quickly cut the signal.

"Oh, my God—what was that?"

Lyla didn't want to know. She grabbed her handbag and ran out of the booth, kicking over the plastic jack-o'lanterns and getting fake cobwebs in her hair. Tim called out for her to stop, but she had to get as far away from that voice as she could. The sound was going to live in her mind forever.

Lyla ran from the building, desperate for something other than the rancid stench of cigarettes and body odor, but the air that greeted her was ice cold. Monochrome clouds threatened rain and the encroaching wind sacrificed autumn leaves to the ground below.

Everywhere Lyla looked, Halloween was beginning to make itself known, and after hearing that voice in the studio, the thought of Halloween terrified her—for the first time in her life.

She left the street for the car park, unlocked her Prius, and climbed inside. She took long, deep breaths in a bid to calm herself, to block out the howling voice, but the wind buffeting the car sounded all too familiar.

"Goddamnit— it wasn't real! Just some guy playing a stupid prank. Get over yourself!"

A check of her watch showed she was going to be late for the seminar if she didn't get on the freeway soon. She started the car and left the car park for the road, merging into traffic. Focusing on the traffic calmed her, but as she started to merge into the right lane to enter the freeway, a fresh gust of wind smothered her car with a vortex of leaves. The hundreds of deathly pale leaves seemed to come out of nowhere, slapping wetly against her windshield and blocking her view. Panicked, Lyla applied the brake and swerved to the left. She heard the blaring of multiple car horns from the drivers around her as the swarm of leaves lifted away to reveal she was about to collide with the rear of another vehicle. Lyla screamed and again swerved hard to the left to avoid the collision, only to strike the guard rail, releasing a hail of sparks and bringing the car to an abrupt stop.

Panting in fear, Lyla scanned the sky, only to find the leaves and the wind had mysteriously vanished.

Lyla's hands wouldn't stop shaking during the Uber ride to the New Hampshire Historical Society Hall. She had to arrange for her Prius to be towed as it had some damage to the suspension and a long scrape down the driver's side, but at least she wasn't hurt. The experience rattled her, the aftermath leaving her with a sickening feeling. Her mouth was dry, her skin clammy. The accident replayed in her head, the leaves twisting over and around the car as if they were attacking her. First the creepy prank caller and then a swarm of leaves. Halloween was turning into a nightmare. The Uber driver pulled up at the hall and Lyla climbed out, only to be greeted by a concerned Renata Dawson.

"Oh, my goodness, Ms. Martin—are you okay?"

Lyla gathered herself and tried to get her bearings. "Yes, I'm fine—I just got a bit of a fright, that's all."

Renata put a hand to her mouth. "Oh, when you called me and said you'd been in an accident I feared the worst. Are you sure you shouldn't go to the emergency department? Get yourself looked at by a doctor? People will understand if you have to cancel."

Lyla shook her head and walked towards the entrance. "No, it's fine. I'd like to just get started."

She entered the hall where about two dozen members of the society were waiting. Mostly retirees, Lyla was astounded that they had nothing better to do than spend their remaining years trying to relive the past. They started clapping as she walked up the stage stairs to the podium. Every year they invited her to come and talk about Halloween and its history in the area and Lyla had always suspected they were using her for pointers on how to write history books of their own. Once the applause ceased, she scanned the crowd, took a deep breath, and began.

"Um, good morning, everyone. I apologize for being late. I had a bit of a mishap on the drive here, but I can assure you that I am perfectly fine. So, without further ado, I'll get started."

She glanced into the crowd. They were all watching her, waiting on her every word. In the back row, however, she noticed an elderly couple and immediately had a feeling that they looked out of place. She turned back to her notes.

"Um, when I started writing my current book—*Halloween Histories*—which is a follow-up to my first book, *Halloween Horrors,* I aimed to dispel some of the myths surrounding Halloween, while also highlighting its rich lore."

Lyla looked at the old couple again and her heart quickened. Their blank faces were gaunt and greying, the flesh stretched taut over the bone. They didn't move, only stared at her from sunken eye sockets. She wanted to turn away, but they held sway over her.

"Take um, one piece of lore around people born on Halloween, for example. As you know, I was born on Halloween in 1962. One of the beliefs was that babies born on Halloween emerged from their mother's wombs wrapped in a fleshy caul. It was also believed that children born on Halloween had what was referred to as "second sight", a psychic ability to see spirits and—"

A loud clatter rang out in the hall, drawing Lyla's gaze directly to the back of the room. The two chairs where the elderly couple had been sitting had toppled over, but the pair was nowhere to be seen. Others in the crowd turned to the back row as Renata picked the chairs up and then shrugged at Lyla in confusion.

*What the hell is going on?* Lyla thought. Had Renata seen the old couple? Had anyone else other than her? She refocused on her presentation.

"Yes, so as I was saying, 'second sight' was—"

Lyla sucked in a sudden breath as her tongue went slack. The words formed in her head, but she had been struck dumb. She stood on the podium, her lips moving without sound. She coughed and poked at her throat, but she was mute. Renata noticed and quickly came to her side.

"Are you all right, Ms. Martin? Do you need a glass of water?"

Renata left the stage and returned with some water a moment later. Lyla took a mouthful and felt her tongue once more.

"Thank…you," she said to Renata before turning to the group. "Not sure what happened there."

Murmurs rose through the crowd, the members concerned with their star presenter's behavior.

"Sorry, everyone. I'll continue. So, 'second sight'… *Tha sinn a" tighinn air son d" anama an nochd*

Lyla had lost control of her words. The gathered crowd frowned and gasped.

*"Fosglaidh am brat ort"*

*"Gus do Ifrinn Oidhche Shamhna a thoirt thugad!"*

Lyla pressed a hand to her temple. The crowd seemed to blur in a haze of distorted color. She didn't know what was happening, but something else had control of her mind and body. Renata came to her again, but the woman's cries of concern were lost in a void. Lyla looked to the exit and saw the elderly couple had moved closer. Their filthy black clothes and gormless faces watching seemed all too familiar. Then Renata's voice broke through.

"Do you need an ambulance?"

Lyla blinked and the elderly couple was gone. She pushed Renata aside and ran for the exit and once she made it outside, she kept running—running for her very soul.

Lyla sat in the back of the taxi with tears streaming down her face. Her day—her Halloween—was inexplicable. Something was reaching for her with icy fingers. The things she had witnessed didn't make sense, but she knew they were real. The voice, the swarm of leaves, the ghosts of her parents, and now something had taken control of her voice.

*Oh, God, my voice. What happened to my voice?*

The driver asked if she was okay, but Lyla ignored him, instead watching out the window to gather her thoughts. The words she'd spoken—or the words that had been spoken through her—she knew to be Gaelic, the ancient language of the

Celts. She'd read some Gaelic during her years of research into the origins of Halloween, but she'd never been able to speak it, or even tried. Lyla removed her glasses and squeezed the bridge of her nose in exhaustion. She tried to recall the Gaelic that had escaped her lips, but it was garbled, like the rest of her head. One of the words did push through: *anama.* She grabbed her phone and searched for the word. The English translation came up as the old Irish word for *soul.*

The voice on the call at the radio station crept back into her mind.

*Her soul.*

Was something truly coming for her soul?

She shivered and closed the phone. Despite her field of research, and upbringing, she'd never truly believed in an afterlife. She saw Halloween as a celebration of remembrance of the dead, a way to soften the dread feelings around mortality and death. The notion of evil spirits had been laughable to her, childish—until now.

The taxi turned into her street and in her shaken state, she'd forgotten that children would be out trick-or-treating. A number of her neighbors had decorated their homes, not knowing a Halloween expert lived just a few doors away. Lyla asked the driver to pull over, paid him, and stepped onto the sidewalk. Small children, draped in white sheets, Spider-Man costumes, and witches' hats were roaming in search of candy, their parents in tow. Lyla weaved through one group to her front gate. She opened it and quickly went inside, locking the door. For the first time in years, there'd be no trick-or-treating at the home of Lyla Martin.

The scotch and soda did little to calm Lyla's nerves. She paced her house and focused on her breathing, but still the fear grew in the pit of her stomach. The sounds of the trick-or-treaters bled in from the outside—laughing children and cackling toy witches, mingling with the chill breeze and flutter of dying leaves.

Lyla tore herself away from the windows, the leaves reminding her too much of the near-fatal accident on the freeway. She sat in a chair and tried to stay calm—to make sense of the day's events. The scotch became sour in her mouth and she thought she was going to throw up. The glass, slick with condensation, slipped from her fingers and splashed on the rug.

"Shit!"

Lyla was bending to pick up the glass when her cell phone rang. She answered it while trying to sop up the spill.

"Lyla, it's Theresa? Are you okay?"

Theresa had been her agent for almost five years. She was the one who'd encouraged her to write *Halloween Horrors.*

"Hi, Theresa—I guess you've heard about my day?"

"Yeah, Tim from 2NGB called. Said you'd stormed out of the interview."

"I didn't storm out! I was…"

"You were what?"

"Look, Theresa, I'm not feeling that well. Can we pick this up tomorrow?"

"I need to catch up with you about your book—the deadline's fast approaching."

Lyla moved to her writing desk to sort through her papers. The printout of the third draft of *Halloween Histories* lay in a large stack near her laptop.

"Okay, yeah, it's coming along. I'll make the deadline."

Lyla flicked through the pages and gasped. The computer-printed text was gone, replaced with a handwritten scrawl. Scratchy handwriting, done with a quill or fingertip. She blocked out Theresa's voice and stared in horror at the macabre screed.

"What the hell?" she said.

"What—what's wrong?" Theresa asked.

She turned the page and the next and the next. Each one was in different handwriting, the writings of madmen and monsters. She couldn't read it, couldn't bear to.

"Someone…someone has written all over my copy of the manuscript."

"What?"

Lyla sat at her desk and started her laptop. She opened the *Halloween Histories* word document and scrolled. The words on the screen transformed before her eyes.

"No!"

"What is going on, Lyla?"

"My manuscript… It's been corrupted or…"

Lyla kept scrolling, each page worse than the last. Then the keys on the keyboard began to type on their own.

*LYLAAA'SSS SSOOOUUULLLLL*

"Oh, God!" Lyla pushed the laptop away and it clattered to the floor, cracking the screen. The fractured text flashed again and again. "No! No, leave me alone!"

"Lyla? Jesus, what's going on?!"

A knock at the door startled Lyla and she dropped the phone. Through the window in the door, she saw three trick-or-treaters, adults wearing elaborate monster outfits. Lyla had never seen such detail in Halloween costumes before.

"Go away!" Lyla cried.

The first trick-or-treater, who wore a skeleton suit, reached up with a bony hand to knock forcefully. As she looked at him, the bones of his suit seemed to yellow and age, become real. The other two—a demon and a witch—gazed at Lyla with cold grey eyes. The skeleton kept knocking.

"I…I'm not accepting trick-or-treaters!"

The skeleton reached down to turn the handle and open the door. Lyla's blood ran cold. *How? How is the door unlocked?*

The skeleton staggered into the room, its bony feet scraping across the tiled floor. The demon followed, with skin blazing red and tendrils of smoke twisting in its wake. The witch, now draped in scorched black lace, howled at her from a cracked and split, toothless mouth. It pointed a crooked finger toward her.

"LYLA'S SOUL!"

Lyla screamed. She backed away as the trio advanced, their visages contorted in hunger. Behind them, seated in Lyla's living room, were the elderly couple—her mother and father, watching in reverence. They'd come to see their daughter dragged off to the land of the dead, on Lyla's last Halloween.

"The name's Crispin – Mister Crispin!"

# VAUDEVILLE

## 1

One year had passed since Anthony Moore's father was found hanging from an oak tree in Keaton Woods.

Anthony lost not only a father, but a piece of his soul. The entire town of Keaton became a void, its citizens orbiting aimlessly around a black hole that was born screaming from that one tree. Anthony understood why the people of Keaton felt his father's death as profoundly as he did; Dominic Moore was a decent man, pleasant, kind, always willing to offer help to anyone who needed it.

Dominic was the sole breadwinner in the Moore family, working at the steel mill in the outskirts of town. He worked hard and every paycheck went back into the mortgage and onto the dinner table.

Anthony remembered the time his father took him to the steel mill; he was about eight years old. It was loud, deafeningly loud. The smell of engine grease was thick and huge machines sliced through sheets of steel like they were butter. Anthony remembered the smiles on the faces of the men his father worked with; they were all like his father—strong, dependable and a little bit mischievous. That day was the greatest day of Anthony's life and he would never forget it. By showing Anthony how to crush cans and bend steel with the push of a button, Dominic forged a kinship with his son that could never be broken—even in death.

Yet it was that same day, four years on, when the bond was

severed; when Anthony experienced the worst day of his life.

He was at school, learning about the forefathers, when Sheriff Dawson came a-calling. At first, Anthony's classmates thought he was in trouble, that he'd stolen something from the general store or thrown a rock at a window. The Sheriff stood in the doorway to the classroom, ten-gallon hat in his hand, pale-faced. Never had the children dreamed of the horrible tragedy he was about to tell.

"It's yer daddy," the Sheriff told the boy in the schoolyard.

Those three words; they carried the same weight as the three other words he'd often heard his mom and dad say to each other.

Flash forward one year where Anthony sat in his bedroom, staring at the only photograph he had of the two of them together. Their smiles could have lit up the world. Again, the boy's thoughts were wrenched back to the remainder of the Sheriff's painful monologue:

"Yer daddy," he muttered. "He's at the hospital, son."

Anthony had asked if his father was okay; if there had been an accident at the mill.

"No, son, he wasn't at the mill. He'd gone out into the woods."

This didn't make sense to Anthony and he asked why.

"No one really knows why, son," the Sheriff said. "They found him in the woods and he was hurt…real bad."

Anthony asked for his mother, wondering why she wasn't at the school to tell him herself.

"Yer momma's with yer daddy. She asked me to come get ya."

Anthony noticed tears in the Sheriff's grey eyes. Since when did a Sheriff cry?

"Sorry, son. It's just such a shock. Yer daddy, well, he was a damn fine man."

*Was?*

"You need to come with me now, Anthony," the Sheriff said, holding out his hand. "Yer momma needs you."

So much had changed since that day, but his father was still dead. His mother didn't need her son anymore. The void—the all-swallowing loss—had claimed his childhood, too. Anthony reached into an old shoebox and retrieved a second photograph.

It was the same photograph, but it hadn't been cropped. In it were Anthony and his father, smiling, embraced in a bear hug against a wheat field bathed in sunshine. To their left, his mother, Madeline, glowing and raven-haired, shared in the embrace. Her smile could have lit up the entire universe.

Madeline Moore hadn't smiled once in a whole year.

"Anthony?"

The boy quickly slipped the photographs back into the shoebox and scampered over to his wardrobe. He stretched up on his tiptoes to place the box on the top shelf and covered it under a blanket.

"Anthony!"

He ran to his bedroom door and closed it behind him.

"Where are you? "

"I'm here, Momma!"

"Get down here!"

Madeline's sweet voice had died not long ago, replaced by a grating resentment towards life; a voice torn apart by the bitter taste of prolonged grief. Anthony ran down the stairs to the kitchen where he found his mother seated at the dinner table, glass in her right hand. Anthony could smell the contents of the glass from where he stood.

"Where have you been, boy?" she said, looking at him through threads of her tainted grey hair. The skin around her eyes was swollen.

"In my room, Momma," Anthony said.

"In my room." A slight grimace passed Madeline's lips before she parted them to take in more of that foul liquid. When she'd swallowed, she said, "You spend too much time in your room."

"Yes, Momma."

Madeline put the glass down, the chink of its contact with the table echoing in the silence.

"I need you to go the store," she said. "We need bread and milk, baloney and eggs for dinner."

"Baloney? Again?" Anthony squirmed. He instantly knew he'd made a mistake.

"Do you want to cook now?" Madeline's eyes suddenly narrowed, spiteful. "Do you want to take over the running of this household? You'll have to become a man before that happens! Walk a mile in your father's—"

She cut the tirade short, turning her gaze to the banister in the living room—to the silver urn that rested there—and back to the vacant glass. She stood up from the chair; Anthony saw she was still wearing her dressing gown.

"You get down to that store and you get what we need." She tossed a twenty-dollar bill on the table. "And you bring me back the change."

"Yes, Momma."

Like a hare fleeing the crosshairs, Anthony grabbed the money and ran for fresh air, for salvation in the sunshine.

Madeline emptied the glass and scanned the kitchen for the bottle. She had to numb the pain and quiet the voice in her head, the voice that had called to her each and every day.

She stood and turned to the kitchen cupboard, remembering she always kept a spare bottle on the top shelf. She pushed aside the plain flour and pasta and glimpsed the sheen of dulled glass at the back, her fingertips meeting its cold touch.

*You need to stop.*

She winced as the voice bled into her mind. *It's just your conscience—has to be,* she told herself. She pulled the bottle from its resting place and unscrewed the lid in desperation. *Please, God, let me wash it all away.*

*Is this how you cope now, by drowning your sorrow?*

She squeezed her eyes shut and swallowed the liquor in one gulp, like a child forced to take medicine. In a few minutes the voice would begin to fade, the vodka dulling it the same way the ocean does a cliff-face.

*You need to listen.*

*Am I going insane? Is that why I yell at Anthony all the time and scold him for the slightest thing?* She poured another glass, turned back to the dinner table and slumped into the chair. The morning sun was glinting off its surface, almost as if it was mocking her.

She had to stay mad at Anthony. It was for his own good. He needed to grow up and take charge because deep down she wasn't sure she had the strength to go on. Her gut twisted with failure and it rose to contort her face with tears. She didn't want to yell at Anthony, but she didn't know how else to talk to him. She didn't want to drink, but she didn't know how to stop the voice. Mother and son would just have to stay apart if they were to survive.

The tears pulled her down and she dropped her head into her arms, letting the tremor of mourning take her. She cried for her son, herself, and especially her husband, because deep down, she knew they were all dead and gone without him.

## 2

Keaton's town center was only four blocks from Anthony's home. Nine hundred and ninety people lived in Keaton and everyone knew everyone; literally one big happy family. Keaton was the perfect nesting ground: lush and green in spring, apple blossoms floating; a wonderland of ice and snow in winter; blazing hot in summer; fall, a pastiche of golden corn fields and hills cast in bronze. It was perfection, simultaneously wild and tamed; a balance of fair and harsh that the people respected and lived by.

And even when Keaton's children died, the landscape went on.

Keaton had land for agriculture and land for industry. The steel mill was the major economy, employing about two hundred and fifty people. The remainder tilled the fields, growing corn, wheat and apples for the town with plenty left over for distribution interstate. The manufactured steel was exported across the globe and the mill's one claim to fame was that some of its steel had been used to rebuild bridges ravaged by war in the Middle East.

On this day, Anthony went into town. It was a Saturday, and Victory Street was particularly busy, with people at the hardware store, the bakery and the deli. Anthony smiled at old Mr. and Mrs. Reynolds as they came out of the bank; Anthony used to swim in the stream at the back of their acreage. He saw people gossiping outside the post office and a dog sitting and panting in the back of a pickup truck, waiting for its master to return. To an outsider, everything would have looked just fine in Keaton.

Anthony was making a path for the general store, admiring all these sights, when he heard a voice call from the road:

"Well, hey there, Anthony."

The boy turned and saw Sheriff Dawson at the wheel of his police cruiser, smiling at him from behind a pair of aviator-style sunglasses.

"Hi, Sheriff," Anthony said as he approached the cruiser. Deputy Thomas Burke was in the passenger seat.

"Hey, Anthony," the Deputy said, with a slight nod.

"Hello, Mr. Burke."

"What you doin' today?" the Sheriff asked.

"I'm running some errands for Momma."

The Sheriff frowned. "How is yer momma these days?"

Anthony paused and glanced at the sidewalk. "She's okay."

"And you?"

"I'm okay, Sheriff."

Even with the sunglasses, Anthony knew the Sheriff was looking right through his lie. The Sheriff reached out his broad right hand to scratch at the boy's hair.

"Well, you get on now, you little scamp—yer momma will be wondering where you got to."

The cruiser drove away and Anthony hoped he was convincing enough not to warrant a visit from the Sheriff at home—his momma wouldn't appreciate that one bit. Anthony went into the general store and smiled at the dentist, Mr. Ogilvy, Barbara Bentley the librarian, and the Cole family who were all crowded around the pastry counter choosing a birthday cake. He went straight to the main counter and found Mrs. Davis, the co-owner, smiling down at him, her jowly face so welcoming.

"Why, it's Anthony Moore," she said. "It's so good to see you."

Anthony blushed. He fished the twenty dollars from his pants pocket and placed it on the counter. "Hello, Mrs. Davis. I'd like to buy some milk and bread and baloney and a dozen eggs please."

Mrs. Davis nodded and put down the copy of *Reader's Digest* she'd been engrossed in. "Okay, then. Will that be all you need?"

"Mm-hmm."

As Mrs. Davis walked off to collect the groceries, Anthony

made a cursory glance around the store. All eyes were upon him. He only knew them all by name, but they could have known him inside out—they had seen into his soul. Yet their gazes were not judgemental, just mournful. He'd love to see them all smile again; even Mrs. Davis's smile seemed…forced. If only they could be happy, then maybe he could finally let go.

On the walls were old photos of the store being built, a newspaper clipping of Mr. and Mrs. Davis celebrating their forty-fifth wedding anniversary, and a giant-sized map of Keaton and its surrounds, complete with a cartoon of the elusive and apparently mystical catfish of Grantham Lake. But there was one item that always piqued Anthony's interest—a small and yellowed photograph that depicted a group of Civil War soldiers camping beside a vast woodland, presumably Keaton Woods. The straight-faced soldiers were interesting enough, but it was the object in the distance behind them that really fascinated Anthony—a large wooden caravan with the words *All-American Travelling Troubadours* painted on the side.

As he gazed at it, Mr. Davis finished up a sale and approached the boy.

"How's your mom doing? I haven't spoken to her in many a while now."

The boy sighed; would telling him the truth make everyone stop asking? No, he had to make them smile.

"She's good," he said.

"Aw, that's good to hear," the old man chuckled lightly. "You looking at my photos, are you?"

"I like the one with the soldiers," Anthony said.

"Interesting, isn't it? There were many Confederate soldiers here during the Civil War. They were planning on making Keaton a fort town, did you know that? But then all of sudden the war was over."

Anthony pointed at the caravan. "Do you know anything about that?"

Mr. Davis picked up the photo frame and scrutinized it over his half-moon glasses. "Gee, I don't know. Looks like a caravan that performers used."

"Performers—like circus performers?"

"Or actors and the like. They were pretty popular in the 1800s."

"Wow," Anthony said.

Mrs. Davis appeared then, a large brown paper bag in her arms.

"Here you go, Anthony, all sorted."

Mr. Davis put the photograph back in its place and checked the items. "Anthony was just telling me his mom's doing well."

"Oh, that's wonderful," Mrs. Davis said. "You tell her 'hi' from us."

Mr. Davis gave Anthony the bag and the change. "Now you just wait a minute there." The old man reached around the counter and plucked a Moon Pie cookie off the shelf. He placed it reverently inside the grocery bag and gave the boy a wink. "On the house," he said.

"Oh, that's lovely, Donald," his wife said.

"Thanks, Mr. Davis," Anthony said.

"My pleasure, son. Now, you get on home, you hear?"

"Yes, sir."

Anthony was grateful for the Davis's kindness and smiles, but deep down he knew they were smiles of sympathy. Didn't they know he was smarter than that? He was almost fourteen—not a little boy any more. They didn't have to lie to him.

He was so deep in thought, his eyes gazing wantonly at the Moon Pie inside the grocery bag, that he never saw the figure walking towards him. A collision was unavoidable. Thankfully, the man caught the paper bag before it hit the pavement. The man, all dressed in black, seemed to bleed into the shadows of the day. Anthony had to look twice before he realized it was Reverend Harris.

"Oh, I'm sorry Anthony—I didn't see you there," he said.

Anthony took the shopping bag back like it was a newborn baby.

"Well, it's certainly been a long time since I've seen you, Anthony Moore," the Reverend said. Well, not since…" He cleared his throat. "How are you, son?"

"I'm okay—and Momma's okay, too," Anthony said with a hint of annoyance.

"That's good, that's good." The Reverend adjusted his collar. "We haven't seen you and your mother at church for a while."

"No, Reverend."

"We'd love to see you—perhaps tomorrow?"

"I'd have to talk to Momma," Anthony said, looking to get past the Reverend.

"Do you think I should come and visit—just to say hello?"

Anthony shrugged and saw a look of desperation in the Reverend's eyes; was he looking for salvation too?

"Could you make her laugh?" the boy asked.

The Reverend chuckled nervously. "Laugh? What do you mean?

"She hasn't laughed in a long time; hasn't even smiled." He stared at the pavement again. "I don't think God's word can help her any more, not unless there's a joke in the Bible."

"Excuse me?" the Reverend said, looking like the boy had slapped him across the face.

Anthony strode away, crossing the road, his arms tight on the bag of groceries. "Sorry, Reverend, but I have to get home."

## 3

The only thing that tormented Anthony about his father's death was the one lingering question: why did he take his own life and leave his family behind?

To try and find an answer to this mystery, to find that release, Anthony would journey every day to the place where his father died. If his mother found out what he did…well, he didn't know what she would do—he hoped she would just send him to his room. Still, he wasn't afraid of the repercussions and Keaton woods didn't scare him either. The woods had become a part of him now, like breathing.

The woods always appeared to be in freeze-frame, not growing in height or depth but thickening in shadow, as if the sun's light found it harder to penetrate with each passing day. The tree trunks soared straight into a dark green canopy, the branches twisting like the matted hair of some hideous beast. In the fall, the leaves were like desiccated skin. Anthony always kept an eye out for them as they tumbled down, lest they land on his head. As he wandered along, the leaves crunched loudly beneath his sneakers.

He followed the track, straining his ears for the sounds of birds or crickets, but there were none. He walked on, his eyes dead ahead, eager to see the tree—the lone tree. It was a Mountain Ash, he'd discovered in the weeks after his father died—he'd read it in a book from the school library. When the grief and loneliness was at its zenith, he searched long and hard for answers in anything.

The tree was at least one hundred feet tall and hundreds of years old. His dad had apparently chosen the lowest branch on which to tie the noose. The bark was grey, with the texture of a burlap sack left in the sun for a hundred years.

As Anthony pictured the tree in his mind, it seemed to will itself into existence, appearing around the bend. His heart began to thrum at the sight of it, a mix of awe and anxiety. Sweat on his pale arms made him shiver. He placed the grocery bag on the ground and stared at the tree. The tree, as usual, looked as if it had been expecting him and for a long time, the two entities—one young, the other old—gazed at one another.

Through the shield of thorns and weeds, they watched the boy. With ebony eyes, they looked him up and down, taking in every square inch of his plump, pink flesh; how he glowed with life.

"He has returned," one of the watchers whispered.

The one to his left held a skeletal finger to his lipless mouth and shushed him through rotted green teeth. "He'll hear us, Rukus. Be silent."

A tall, slender woman, her form forever fixed with lividity, leaned in. She held the frayed edges of her filthy tutu between cold fingers.

"He's so adorable. I just want to squeeze him." She hugged herself to illustrate the point; the thick catgut stitches keeping her arms attached to her torso squeaked under pressure. "Can I hold him? Please, Mister Crispin?"

Mister Crispin, the one with the lipless mouth, whirled on her, his visage abnormally contorted.

"No. Be silent, Celeste!"

Rukus, Celeste and the other accompanying creature backed away, fear in their hollow eyes. Mister Crispin tried to retain their calm by standing tall and adjusting his battered top-hat.

"Please, my kin, we must simply watch and wait."

Rukus looked through the bushes again at the boy and began to fidget with his boater hat. "Why can't we just take him now?"

Crispin whispered in his ear. "He might scream, Rukus. Our appearance is…not very pleasant."

Rukus pondered this and finally nodded in agreement. "Yes, yes," he said. "But this boy could make us whole again. Not many people come into these woods anymore."

Crispin rested a bony hand on Rukus's shoulder. "I understand that, Rukus, but we must have more patience. You all remember the mess that was created the last time we fed—the trouble we had to go to in order to avoid detection?"

All of them were suddenly downcast, the memory flooding into their decaying souls, but Crispin gathered them in close.

"We must be cautious," he told them. "Like the old days. Perhaps we can woo this boy—give him a private performance?"

Crispin's comrades gazed at the boy and smiled with realization—smiles of menace.

"One final show?" Crispin said.

"One final show," Rukus replied with a sneer.

Crispin's teeth shone in the half-light. "Then it's time for makeup!"

## 4

A snap of twigs brought Anthony out of his reverie and he discovered he was not alone.

Four people had emerged unseen from the woods; immediately, the boy's young mind filled with the desire to run. The quartet were dressed as if they were about to join the circus and bared garish smiles.

The tallest of them, a man in a top-hat and dark velvet coat, led the pack. Behind him stood a beautiful woman with bleached blonde hair, wearing a pink lace tutu and glittering tiara. There was another man in a candy-striped vest and boater hat, and the last man wore a black tuxedo and white gloves.

"Who are you?" Anthony asked.

The man in the top-hat outstretched his hand. "The name's Crispin—Mister Crispin!" He turned to his entourage. "And these are my friends: Charlie Rukus, Celeste Renoir and The Great Kaskaraken!" Rukus gave a bow and Celeste offered a curtsy. Kaskaraken seemed indifferent. "What's your name, lad?" Crispin asked.

Anthony scanned the woods. "Where did you come from?"

Crispin clapped his hands and looked to his friends. "You see? I told you this lad's a real bright spark! He'd be perfect for our show!"

Anthony frowned. "Show? What show?"

Rukus stepped forwards, his arms wide, white cane pointing to the sky.

"The Show of the Century!" he said. "Oh, there'll be singing and dancing and magic with The Great Kaskaraken!"

Anthony took a step back. "Magic?"

"Yes," Kaskaraken said, his baritone voice startling the boy. "Would you like to see a magic trick, little one?"

"You can do real magic?"

"Indeed," Kaskaraken said, his expression deadpan.

"You'd like to see The Great Kaskaraken perform a magic trick, wouldn't you, lad?" Crispin chimed in, suddenly kneeling down to be face to face with the boy.

Anthony looked at the man's face—into his eyes—and cringed. The color of his irises seemed…unnatural.

"I don't know," he said.

"Oh, come on lad, it'll be fun!" Rukus said.

Anthony considered the strangers: Rukus ogled him; the beautiful Celeste offered him a wink; Crispin's smile seemed to stretch his face beyond normal measure; and The Great Kaskaraken could have been a statue. The boy wondered why they would all be wearing such bizarre costumes out here in the middle of the woods. Even more mysterious was why he'd never seen them in the woods before.

"Do you live here—in the woods, I mean?" Anthony said.

"Yes and no," Crispin replied. "We're just passing through."

"Like travelers?"

Crispin pinched Anthony's cheek. It stung. "Oh, you're as sharp as a pin, you are! You're right—we are troubadours; performers. We go from town to town and entertain the people." He put a hand to his chest. "I'm the master of ceremonies, or the host. Rukus is like, well, a court jester, and Kaskaraken and Celeste put on a magic show."

For some reason the old photograph in the Davis's general store came to mind. "So, you're like a circus?"

"In a way, yes, but we perform on the stage—in a theater. Understand?"

Anthony nodded. "I think so. So, are you going to perform in Keaton then?"

Crispin leaned in closer; Anthony noticed the man hadn't brushed his teeth in a long while. "We'd like to, but we need to practice first," Crispin said. "Would you like to help us with that?"

"Me?"

"You could tell your young friends about us, get them to come?" Rukus said.

"We only need four, sugar," Celeste added.

"Why only four?"

Crispin put a hand on Anthony's shoulder; there was no warmth in his touch. "Well, there are only four of us," he said. "We like to make our practice performances very special. Very personal. Do you think you can help us?"

Anthony thought long and hard. He didn't like the look of these strangers or the fact that they appeared to be hiding in the woods. What was stopping them from coming into town?

"Why just kids—aren't adults allowed?" he asked.

"You ask so many questions for someone so young," Crispin said with a chuckle. "You know what adults can be like these days—all work and no play. Our show is meant for children to enjoy."

Anthony scratched his head. "I'm not sure the kids' parents

would let them come here on their own."

A flash of anger crossed Crispin's face and Anthony swore he glimpsed a change in the skin, like something broken underneath, attempting to come through.

"Here's a question for you, lad—what are you doing here on your own in our woods every damn day?"

Anthony took another step back and almost tripped over his own feet. Crispin's voice was not just loud, it was more guttural, resembling a growl. The boy was now genuinely afraid. He knew nothing about these so-called "troubadours"—he didn't even know what the word meant—and he wasn't about to reveal anything about himself. His father taught him early on about stranger danger.

"I just…come here for a walk…that's all."

"Liar!" Rukus cried, giving Anthony a start. "You come here to look at the tree, don't you?"

Crispin whirled on Rukus. "Shut your filthy mouth!"

Rukus cringed, but he was lucky that his master turned his attention back to Anthony. Anthony began to back away with a series of rapid steps as Crispin flashed him that foul smile.

"I have to go now," the boy said.

"Come now, lad, stay a while longer," Crispin said. "We don't even know your name."

Anthony shook his head and broke into a run, desperate to escape the woods and its strangers. He was young and fast, but somehow Crispin's voice kept up the pace, resounding inside his tiny mind.

*Don't you want to see your daddy again?*

Anthony stopped dead, his feet stirring up the carpet of leaves. Heart pounding in his ears, he turned around to face them. The troubadours had changed; their clothing was now torn and bloody. Mister Crispin's face was a pastiche of scars flaring red, and the very top of his tall hat blazed with fire. Rukus's candy stripes were bleeding down his white trousers and his eyes bulged with the pressure of putrefaction. Celeste resembled an artist's mannequin, her arms, legs and head were held together tenuously with stitches. The Great Kaskaraken floated several feet off the ground, his body emitting a sickening green luminescence.

Anthony wanted to scream for his mother, but the mention of his father—and the sight of these horrific beings—left him mute.

Crispin smiled, the charred muscles of his cheeks pulling his gums taut. He held out his hand.

"We can take you to him, lad," he said. "We know just where to find him. All you have to do is help us put on our best ever show."

## 5

Tears streamed down Anthony's cheeks as he ran back home. They were tears of shock and terror and when he wiped them from his face, he hoped he was wiping away the horrible visions he had witnessed just minutes before.

After one whole year, Anthony had finally seen his father again—or rather his father's soul.

The monster Mister Crispin had the power to reunite the living and the dead.

Anthony squeezed his eyes shut and saw his father's ragged ghost in his mind's eye. Dominic Moore was a dim shade, in a cage; a whisper in the dark. Anthony could still see the desperation in his father's ethereal gaze, and when he spoke to his son for the first time since he'd died, all he said was:

RUN.

So, Anthony did, but not before Mister Crispin and his troupe offered him a proposition: bring the monsters four young souls or they'd finish his daddy off.

Mister Crispin revealed the truth in all its grotesque detail; how one year ago, Dominic Moore had entered the woods and the troubadours had attacked him—murdered him—just to take his soul. How they'd strung up his corpse in a tree. The truth burned in Anthony's soul with the fury of a furnace and he just wanted to die.

But then he remembered he'd seen his father again—a remnant of him, but his father nonetheless.

He stopped running when he reached Forest Road, the main

thoroughfare from the woods into Keaton town. He sucked in a multitude of breaths, trying to steady his fear-stricken heart.

*What do I do now?*

As his mind steadily cleared, Anthony began to doubt what he'd seen. Was it just what he wanted to see? The troupe had seemed so real and the sudden reconnection with his father had reignited that familiar ache of loss. How could that be faked?

*What do I do?*

If he did what the monsters wanted, children would die, but then he would see his father again.

Should he tell his mother? He gritted his teeth; she would never believe him. He was just a boy—a lonely little boy trying to deal with the fact he had no father figure. No, telling her would just make her angry.

Should he tell the Sheriff? No, the Sheriff would just tell his mom.

*I don't know what to do.*

He stood at the edge of the woods and stared at his tiny home town, plagued with doubt. Then he felt a cold hand on his shoulder. He gave out a cry when he turned and saw the Great Kaskaraken behind him. His slick-backed ebony hair and needle-thin moustache were stark against his deathly face. He held out a white-gloved hand and, with a flick of his wrist, produced four slips of paper.

"You forgot your tickets to the show," Kaskaraken said. The demon magician reached down, took Anthony's right hand, and placed the tickets tenderly in his sweaty palm. "Ensure you give these to your friends."

Then he was gone, as if the air itself had devoured him. The horrible display of magic made Anthony run anew.

"Where the hell are the groceries?" Madeline said.

Anthony stood in the doorway, chest heaving from exertion. He'd left the grocery bag in the woods—with the monsters.

"I…I dropped it," he said.

"Dropped it. Dropped it where?" For a moment, his mother's mouth could have belonged to Mister Crispin.

Anthony racked his brain for an imaginary answer, but all he could see was Mister Crispin's laughing rag of a face and his father's distant eyes.

"I was…walking back and I…tripped over," he said. "The eggs broke and…"

His mother took a step towards him and put her hands on her hips. Anthony could feel her rage, smell the liquor in her sweat.

"So, you just threw them away, wasted all that money?"

Anthony rummaged in his pockets and pulled out the change. "I got the change…" he began, but Madeline lashed out and grabbed the money from his sweaty palm before he could utter another word.

"And what have I got to show for the money I just spent, huh? Nothing! I asked you to do one simple job, Anthony, and you just went and screwed it up!"

"I'm sorry, Momma!" Anthony's voice was choked with tears.

"Just go to your room. You stay there until I call you for dinner—whatever that's going to be!"

Anthony ran up the stairs, keen to avoid any further scolding and especially any further questions about why he was late—where he'd been. He had to ensure she never knew about the woods and the horrible secrets that dwelled there.

Mashed potatoes and beans for dinner, garnished with silence and animosity.

Madeline didn't want to speak to her son and Anthony was grateful. He ate his meal slowly; he didn't want to give his mother any reason to chide him, to suspect anything. She was angry at him, but only because he'd dropped the groceries, not because he'd been communing with the dead.

When they both cleared their plates, she sent him to his room for the rest of the night, telling him only that he had to think about what he'd done. He nodded, ambled up the stairs to his room and closed the door. Minutes later, he heard the television come on, knowing his mother would surely fixate upon it until she fell asleep or passed out—whichever came first.

Anthony climbed into bed with the photograph of his father

and cried. The helplessness he felt seeped out of his soul onto his face, lost in the fraying threads of his pillow. Thankfully, the flow of despair put him to sleep and dulled the fear that would ultimately arise anew with dawn.

## 6

When Anthony awoke on Monday morning, he found his mother passed out in the recliner, a drained scotch glass perched unsteadily in her palm. The boy removed the glass gently and glanced at the television, which was still on; the morning presenters were sharing a joke with a seemingly perfect and well-adjusted audience.

Very quietly, Anthony placed the glass in the kitchen basin and set about getting ready for the school day. He made himself toast and juice, munching on it while he prepared a lunch of peanut butter and jelly sandwiches and an apple.

Secretly, and for the first time, Anthony thanked God for his mother's alcohol-induced lethargy; it meant he could leave the house and prepare for the grim task ahead. He packed the meagre lunch in his schoolbag, ensured the four tickets were in his pocket, and then sat down to write his mother a note:

*Momma,*

*Gone to school. Made my own lunch.*

*I'm sorry about the groceries.*

*Anthony*

He left the note on the dinner table and gave his mother one last look. He felt like he was about to betray the entire world—his entire existence—but he had to set his father free and maybe, just maybe, he would set his mother free, too.

And with that hope in his heart, he closed the front door behind him.

The only contingency Anthony hadn't factored in to completing the monsters' task was the fact that he didn't really have any friends at school.

He knew very few of his classmates by name, but since his father's death he had isolated himself from contact with anyone. Now he needed to reach out to them and he had no idea where to start.

Anthony sat in a stall of the boy's toilets and stared at the tickets. They felt brand new; like real tickets to a real stage show. He began to worry about what would happen to the children he gave them to, but he worried more about what would happen to his father if he didn't. He got up off the seat and flushed to complete the illusion he was simply answering the call of nature. He left the stall, washed his hands and exited the bathroom into a hallway packed with grade schoolers.

He could feel their eyes upon him as he weaved his way to the classroom. Their stares said it all: *That's the boy whose dad hanged himself; they say his mom's a drunk; they've got no money; he's a loser, a freak, a nobody.* Each and every one of them would have been thinking the same thing. He didn't think any of them would give him the time of day, let alone accept tickets to a strange performance in the middle of Keaton Woods.

Anthony sat at his desk and, keeping his head low, scanned his classmates. There were more girls than boys—girls didn't like him. Of the boys, most were of the athletic variety—football jocks or sprinters in the making.

Then, amidst the crowd, he saw a glimmer of hope.

The boy was bone-thin and short, a long, straight fringe dangling over horn-rimmed glasses. He seemed silently eager for class to begin, taking his seat and resting his hands atop his stack of workbooks. Anthony didn't know who this boy was, but he decided he would approach him at first break. Surely, despite outward appearances, this boy would like stage shows—and perhaps even know of other children who liked them too.

Anthony gingerly approached the boy as he sat under a tree in the schoolyard, engrossed in a tattered book.

"Hey," Anthony said.

The boy looked up from the page and Anthony attempted a smile, but it felt awkward.

"Hello," the boy said and closed his book.

"What you reading?"

Anthony saw him scrunch up his nose; at first, he thought he was about sneeze, until he realized it was a way of keeping his heavy, horn-rimmed glasses in place.

"Tom Sawyer," the boy said.

Anthony examined the cover of the book, which depicted two boys fishing, pieces of straw dangling from their lips.

"That's an adventure one, right—on a big river?" he asked.

"The Mississippi," his classmate confirmed.

This time, the boy gave in and used his finger to reposition his glasses. "You're in my English class, aren't you?"

"Yeah, my name's Anthony. Anthony Moore."

Anthony saw the interplay of thought on the boy's face. He wondered if he knew who he was—who his father was.

"Donald Boysie's my name," he said. "I remember the day the Sheriff came in looking for you."

Anthony went silent, thinking of his father in the woods with the monsters taunting him. He saw Donald staring at him and imagined he was thinking *what a weirdo!* Anthony wondered now whether he'd made a mistake even talking to Donald, but then he thought of his task and how much he needed a new friend. He sat down next to Donald, an act which took both of them by surprise.

"So, you like adventures, then?" Anthony said.

Donald shrugged. "I like reading, mostly."

"How would you like to have a real adventure—some real fun?"

"What do you mean?"

"What if..." Anthony tried hard to display excitement and not fear. "What if I shared a secret with you?"

"A secret?"

"What if I knew about a fun place no one else did."

Anthony was pleased to see Donald's eyes light up. "Like what?"

"Like my own private circus."

"Really?"

"Well, it's not actually a circus—it's more like a group of, umm, play-actors."

Anthony saw Donald frown and the action sent his glasses down his nose again; he pushed them back up. "I don't understand," he said. "How would you have your own group of performers?"

Anthony averted his gaze. "They're not mine, I met them outside town. They've just arrived and they need to practice before they put on their big show."

Donald scratched at his ridiculously straight hair in thought. "So, they're rehearsing?"

"Yeah, rehearsing."

"What do they do?"

"Umm, magic tricks and stuff. Some dancing, too. So, would you like to come and meet them or not?" Anthony reached into his pocket and retrieved a slip of paper. "They gave me some tickets."

He handed it to Donald, who gasped at the fancy script printed in red ink:

> VAUDEVILLE!
>
> *Come one, come all and see the All-American Travelling Troubadours starring:*
>
> *Mister Crispin! Charlie Rukus! Celeste Renoir and The Great Kaskaraken!*
>
> CHILDREN FREE!

"When is it happening?" Donald said, eyes even wider.

"Umm, tonight. After school," Anthony said. "So, will you come?"

Anthony watched as dismay wiped the excitement from Donald's face.

"Tonight? Gee, I'd have to ask my mom—"

Anthony's arm shot out and gripped Donald's. "No! You can't tell anyone!"

"Why not?" Donald said, pulling his arm free.

Anthony bit his lip to prevent any further outbursts and checked there was no one in earshot before he said, "Hey, come on. I'm sorry, okay? I didn't mean to scare you. It's just that, well, they told me only to bring kids. They want it to be a surprise for the grownups."

Donald swallowed. "Okay, but I'm still not sure—"

"You've got to see these guys. Kaskaraken made a whole pack of cards disappear and Miss Celeste is real pretty. Come on. Please?"

Anthony watched Donald stare at the ticket for what seemed like forever. Surely the idea of seeing a circus was enticing; he would have jumped at the chance.

"My dad doesn't like me going to circuses," Donald said finally. "I think I went to one once when I was three, but then it was all about going to school and getting a good education. I'm not even supposed to have friends."

Anthony felt sorry for Donald, but secretly was glad. "Every kid should see a circus when it's in town," he said.

"You're right," Donald said, but then he turned serious. "I'll come, but only for a little while—I don't want my mom or dad wondering where I am."

Anthony's entire face was changed by his smile. "Great!" he said. "But hey, do you know anyone else who'd like to come? I've got three more tickets!"

## 7

Anthony didn't really take notice of girls, but he had to admit that Donald's sister Catherine could have been considered pretty. Yet Anthony knew as soon as Donald interrupted his sister's gossip session with her friends that she had little consideration for boys their age. Anthony winced as Catherine Boysie immediately began to berate her brother in front of everyone.

"I thought I told you not to bother me during lunch," she told Donald.

"I just wanted to ask you something," Donald said, adjusting his glasses.

Anthony heard Catherine sigh heavily and he guessed this was how sister-and-brother relationships ran—a fully requited love-hate relationship.

"What is it, and make it quick," she said, dragging Donald away from her giggling friends by the shirt sleeve.

Anthony flinched when Donald turned and pointed to him.

"Well, my friend Anthony has invited me to a special show

and I have some extra tickets and I thought you might like to come?"

Anthony watched Catherine study him and he'd never felt so small. Instinctively, he pushed out his chest and tried to look tough.

"Anthony?" she said, squinting. "Who's he?"

"He's just my friend," Donald said.

"What tickets are you talking about?" She held out her hand until Donald handed over his ticket.

"Vaudeville? What is that, a band?"

Donald chuckled. "No, they're real actors. They're going to perform in Keaton and Anthony got some free tickets when he met them in the woods and he's got three more and I thought you—"

Catherine grimaced. "Me? No. No way!"

"But Anthony says they need four kids—"

Catherine flashed her brother a scornful look. "I'm almost sixteen. I'm not into magic shows and all that. You go to it if you want."

Donald sighed and took the ticket back.

"Have you asked Mom and Dad if you can go?" Catherine called as her brother began to walk away.

"Umm…"

Catherine laughed. "Dad will tan your hide when he finds out what you're up to!"

Anthony saw Donald's face flash with panic. "You won't tell them, will you? It's after school and I thought…if you told them I was in the library studying or something? I'll only be gone for an hour—honest."

Catherine dismissed her brother with a wave. "Fine, whatever."

As they walked away, Anthony couldn't help but feel some sympathy for Donald. "What's her problem?"

"She's just sixteen, that's all. Come on, let's go."

Catherine wouldn't have given them a second thought if it wasn't for the look her friend Cherise was giving her.

"What?" Catherine said, instinctively checking her hair.

"Where's your brother going with that weirdo?" Cherise said.

"Oh, he's made a new friend," Catherine said. "Finally, he might stop bugging me. They're running off to the woods to see some magic show or something."

"The woods?" Cherise gasped.

"Yeah, so what?"

"Don't you know who that other boy is?"

Catherine shook her head; Cherise's worried look became infectious.

"That's Anthony Moore," Cherise said. "You know, the boy whose father hanged himself last year—in the woods!"

And all of a sudden, Catherine wished Donald was bothering her again.

The sun was falling steadily towards twilight when Anthony and Donald set off for Keaton woods.

Donald's excitement quickly began to annoy Anthony, the way he seemed to skip with each step. He wished he could just drag Donald into the woods and let the monsters take him, but he couldn't be like them. If only things were different—if only he could have known Donald under different circumstances. Instead, he would have to pretend they were going to have the time of their lives.

"So, tell me more about these performers?" Donald asked.

"Huh?"

"The vaudeville people—what are they like?"

Anthony conjured his latest lie as if it was second nature. "Umm, they're nice," he said. "Real friendly, like."

"Then why do you look so worried?"

Anthony stopped walking and stared at him. "No, I'm not."

"Is it because we haven't got the four? Will they be upset or something?"

Anthony sighed and shivered; the deception was getting on his nerves. "I hope not. Come on, we'd better keep going before it gets too dark."

Donald caught up. "So, what are they like then?"

"I don't know."

"What do you mean you don't know? You're the one who's met them already."

Anthony picked up his pace.

"Yeah, I know I've met them."

"Then what do they look like?"

Anthony stopped short again and whirled on Donald, anger knotting his blond eyebrows together.

"Why do you keep asking questions? They don't like questions, okay!"

Donald flinched. "You asked me to come. I just want to know what they look like. I don't know why you're so mad with me."

Anthony turned his eyes to the ground, scuffing the dirt with the toe of his sneaker. When he eventually lifted his gaze, he fought the tears welling up in his eyes.

"Look, I'm sorry," Anthony said. "I guess I'm just nervous, that's all. I think it would be better if you just met them yourself."

Anthony turned and waited; would Donald run away? Deep down, he hoped so. Then he heard his friend jog towards him.

"Okay. I'm sorry, too."

They walked in silence for a few minutes and Anthony watched Donald gaze at the trees of the woods emerging on the horizon, bathed in the orange glow of the setting sun.

"Were you in the woods because of your dad?" Donald asked.

Anthony turned, frowning. "What?"

"When you met the performers?"

Anthony pictured the terrible quartet crawling out of the bushes towards him just hours before. He nodded, almost unconsciously.

"Did you tell them that's why you were there—did you tell them about your dad?" Donald pried further.

Anthony swallowed hard. "Yeah, that's why they gave me the tickets. They wanted to cheer me up by putting on a show, I guess."

Donald smiled. "That's nice."

"Yeah. Come on, they'll be waiting."

Anthony wanted to tell Donald to run, to tell him not to believe a single word he had to say. He wanted to shout the truth about what resided in the woods and share his fear with Donald, but all he could see in his heart was his father—that one vision clouded any sense of reason. He heard Donald's footfalls behind him; if only his newfound friend knew what he was walking into. Yet, it was too late now—the monsters were just around the corner.

"I've only been in these woods a few times, when I was little," Donald told him, but his voice was swallowed quickly by the silence.

Anthony was mute with trepidation, but Donald kept on talking.

"They're kind of creepy even in the daytime."

Anthony's feet dragged in the dirt, while Donald gazed at the trees and back to his companion.

"Do you think your dad's here?"

Donald's words were cut short as a figure suddenly emerged from behind an ash tree. Both boys gasped at the man in the top hat and coat tails—the enigmatic Mister Crispin. He was wearing his human visage—and a wide smile.

"Hello there, boys!" Crispin said.

Anthony saw Donald look to him for some confirmation, but he never gave a hint of response; he simply stared at his father's captor, wearing an expression that gave nothing away.

Donald turned and offered Mister Crispin a smile. "Are you one of the performers?"

Crispin threw his arms wide. "Oh, yes. Mister Crispin at your service!" He shook Donald's hand enthusiastically. "I hope you're ready for the big show."

Anthony stayed straight-faced as Donald nodded and smiled; the boy was under Crispin's spell now.

"The rehearsal?" Donald asked.

Crispin snapped his fingers. "Exactly, my boy!" Then his jocularity seemed to bleed from his face. "Although, I fear there may be something amiss." He turned his eyes to Anthony, who began to tremble.

"Anthony, what's wrong?" Donald said.

Crispin stepped past Donald and bent to peer into Anthony's

terrified eyes. "Where are the rest of the children?"

"I'm sorry," Anthony said.

"You're sorry?" Crispin snapped, his outburst startling Donald.

"I couldn't find anyone else, only him."

Crispin turned to consider Donald and there was such darkness in the performer's eyes that his young blood ran cold. "Him?" Crispin said. "One solitary boy?" He turned back to Anthony. "I said four! Four children! Was that really too much to ask?" He reached out and gripped Anthony's shoulder. The boy winced. "Two of you is not enough. I need four!"

Anthony began to cry. "I said I was sorry."

"I tried to get my sister to come," Donald said, a mixture of confusion and fear on his impish face. "But she said she was too old for a magic show. It's not Anthony's fault, sir."

Crispin reached out his other hand and took Donald in a half embrace. He brought the two friends together and Anthony's fear seemed to close the space between them. They could suddenly smell Crispin—a deep, strong aroma of mold and dust. His clothes, for an instant, appeared to be falling apart.

"It's no matter," Crispin told them. "We'll just make do with what we have, won't we? Two can easily be divided into four. Shall we meet the others?"

As if on cue, Rukus, Celeste and The Great Kaskaraken appeared, born from the shadows. Anthony saw that all of them seemed agitated; pre-occupied with some secret need.

"Did I hear Anthony correctly?" Rukus said, with a sneer. "That he has only brought along one other?" He tsked and tapped his cane incessantly on the ground.

"Oh, dear," Celeste added, but she too seemed to seethe with a tempered fury.

"What shall we do now, Mister Crispin?" Kaskaraken said, his impatience hanging over him as heavily as his cloak.

"Can't you put the show on anymore?" Donald asked. Anthony shook his head at him to be quiet.

"Oh, there'll still be a show," Crispin said. "There was always going to be a show. We'll simply have to improvise, won't we, my friends?"

Rukus chuckled, his head bobbing in agreement. He licked his lips lasciviously.

"I want to see my dad," Anthony said.

Anthony saw the complete bewilderment in Donald's eyes. "You're dad? What are you talking about? He's…dead."

Rukus suddenly burst out laughing, a hideous wet cackle. "Oh, he's dead all right! But then again, so are we!"

Donald searched all their faces; Anthony could see his friend wasn't sure if Rukus was joking.

"Don't, please!" Anthony cried as he tried to squirm free of Crispin's grasp.

All the performers began to laugh in unison. The boys watched as Crispin's face started to melt, a fire suddenly erupting from the top of his hat. Rukus began to dance a jig, the candy-stripes of his vest running with fresh, flowing blood. Celeste's throat was slashed by an invisible blade, followed by her arms and luscious legs. Kaskaraken opened his cloak and a great serpent slid out of from his hollow rib cage.

"I want to go home!" Donald shrieked. "I want my mom!"

Crispin wrapped a rotted hand over the boy's mouth and gazed right into his soul, with opaque eyes that swam in blackened sockets.

"You can't leave now, Donald. The show's just about to start and I'm afraid all tickets are non-refundable!"

## 8

Their hands tied together, Anthony and Donald trembled against each other as the All-American Travelling Troubadours set up their grotesque stage in the middle of Keaton woods.

The pair watched through tear-soaked eyes as Kaskaraken conjured the elaborate construction from thin air. With a wave of his hands, thick red velvet curtains rained down, thread after thread. With a snap of his fingers, orbs of iridescent green light pulsed into existence, illuminating the arena. The light and the shadow were in a constant battle for dominance of the stage, players in their own right. Then with a bow to the boys, the unholy magician departed and was replaced by the vile Mister Crispin who trod the floorboards with unrivalled enthusiasm.

The sun was burrowing into the horizon, pushing the creeping shadows ever closer, like skeletal fingers reaching out for salvation. Donald tried desperately to loosen his bonds, but all Anthony could do—or wanted to do—was weep.

"I'm sorry, Donald," Anthony said. "I'm really sorry."

"Did you know they were...monsters?" Donald said, fear shaking his voice.

"Of course he knew!" Crispin called from the stage. "We instructed him to bring children here, but still he failed miserably—so now our little deal is off!"

Donald frowned and fresh tears rolled down his face. "Deal?"

"Your friend Anthony there agreed to bring four new souls for us to feast upon in exchange for the freedom of his dear old daddy!" Crispin explained.

Donald turned to Anthony. "But your dad's dead!"

"Yes, but we kept his soul for dessert," Crispin said, his lipless maw somehow still capable of a smile. "Sadly, Mr. Moore has lost his sweetness and I'm not entirely heartless. Well, almost!" He gestured off stage. "But enough about me... Let's meet the former man himself! Celeste, if you please..."

Celeste Renoir appeared from behind the curtain pushing a great iron cage with a dim specter squatting inside—the ghost of Dominic Moore. He was in the foetal position, fading in and out of reality like an incandescent light bulb about to expire.

"Dad!" Anthony cried.

"Here's your daddy!" Crispin rejoiced. "He'll take center stage during the show, but I'm afraid your indiscretion, Anthony, will cost you. When the show's done, he'll be our first meal!"

"No!" Anthony cried, fighting his bonds.

"Oh, yes, my boy. You just sit back and relax as we present our Tragical History Tour!"

"Wait! Wait!" said a voice from behind them.

Anthony and Donald turned to see Rukus dragging Catherine and another girl from the bushes, his foul mummified hands clamped tight over their mouths.

"Oh, Mister Crispin!" Rukus said, his sing-song voice rising through the trees. "Looks like we've got a few stragglers here, and they don't have their tickets!"

Crispin bounded off the stage, excitement twisting his haggard face to breaking point. He now had his four souls.

"Well, well, well," Crispin chimed. "That's fantastic because there're some spare seats right here in the front row!"

Mister Crispin took a long, low bow and removed his hat to reveal a hairless, fleshless pate. Then slowly, methodically, he straightened and replaced the hat as if he was crowning himself King of the Dead. Then he stared at the children, a gaze that was all at once ferocious, beguiling and stone cold.

Anthony, Donald, Catherine and Cherise were an audience captivated by the fear Crispin generated. Anthony watched Crispin scan their faces; how, with effort, he drew back his gums from his teeth and flames burst from his top hat into the night air. The girls shrieked and the boys trembled. The show had begun.

"Welcome! Welcome!" Crispin began. "Welcome to the All-American Travelling Troubadours Show! Tonight you will be treated to a plethora of delights, both wicked and wild. Your fears will be realized! Your doubts assuaged! Tonight you will peer into the shadows and see—if you dare—the darkness inside yourself!

"I am Theodore Crispin, your host and master of the fire!"

Crispin clicked his fingers and fire engulfed his right hand. The flames twirled and licked at the bones of his blackened fingers, crackling and sparking. He knelt and stretched his arm out towards the children so they could better witness it.

"I imagine you are all wondering how I could perform such a feat?" he said. "Well, stay tuned, my friends, for we shall share all our life stories with you—tales that you will never, ever forget!"

Crispin stood and twirled on the spot and in an instant the flames were gone.

"But first, some light entertainment! I call to the stage our very own mischief maker, Charles Ramsey Rukus!"

Crispin withdrew from the stage with a flurry of bows and Charlie Rukus appeared. There was music, a cacophony of invisible piano and accordion to herald his arrival. The rake-thin undead troubadour launched into a jig, waving his boater hat, twirling his cane.

The children stared at his sickening dance; the way all his joints seemed to loll and roll. He was a demonic doll raving and smiling like a loon.

"Hey-yah! Hey-yah! Hey-yah!" he sang. "Rukus is my name and making a ruckus is my game!"

His jig morphed into a tap, his shoes clacking on the boards in tune with the terrible throng of the children's beating hearts. Rukus reveled in their disgust and his hunger was more prominent than Crispin's, his tongue darting snake-like in and out of his mouth. Anthony turned his face away, instead focusing on the spirit of his father, caged and barren; until Rukus jumped off the stage in front of him with a bouquet of dead daffodils in his gnarled hand.

"What's your name, sonny-jim?" Rukus said, his jaundiced eyes flicking about like a chameleon.

Anthony refused to respond, which only enraged Rukus, who tossed the flowers aside and slapped the boy hard across the cheek.

"I'm talking to you, boy! Didn't yer daddy ever teach you it's impolite to ignore someone when they say hello to you?"

There was a moan from the cage and Rukus turned to see Dominic Moore reaching out to his son from between the bars.

"Oh, yer daddy's right here. Let's ask him ourselves!" Rukus went to move away, but Anthony gripped his sleeve—only to regret it as the candy stripes smeared blood all over his fingers.

"Wait!" Anthony cried. "I'll play. I'll play your game."

Rukus laughed a wet death rattle. "There's no need—I already know yer name! It's Anthony William Moore. Hah!" He moved to Donald and the girls, his hands fidgety. "But it's yer friends here I'm not familiar with." The demon leant down and breathed foulness into Cherise's ear, his eyes leering down her blouse. "What's yer name, sweetie pie?"

"Please don't hurt me!" she sobbed.

Rukus put his lips against her ear. "Then just tell me yer name."

"Just let us go, you animal!" Catherine said.

Rukus whirled on her, his loose jaw almost falling from its decrepit tether. "I beg yer pardon?"

"Just let us go!" Catherine said.

There was a rapid deepening of Rukus"s brow and his eyes lost their gleam. He grimaced so tightly they all thought his lips would split.

"Don't you talk to me like that, you little bitch!" He moved to Catherine in a blur, his ragged fingers grabbing a clutch of her hair. His decay invaded her senses. "How dare you speak to me like that. I was just talking to her, being polite, but you…yer anything but!

"You're hurting me!" Catherine shrieked.

"Leave my sister alone!" Donald said, and Rukus gawped at him in genuine surprise.

"Oh, hello. I didn't see you there!" Rukus released his grip of Catherine and strode over to the boy. Donald tried to back away, but all four children were tied tight together. "You're her little brother, aren't you?" Rukus asked.

"Yes," Donald sniffed.

"Donnie, don't!" his sister said.

Rukus turned to her, his rakish finger pressed to his lips; then when she was silent his eyes shifted back to Donald.

"Now, you just go ahead and tell me yer name," he said. "Go on, you can tell ol' Charlie."

Donald tried to look to the other children for guidance, but he was alone, none of them daring to defy the will of the mad jester.

"Donald," he said finally.

Rukus smiled, genuinely happy, his green teeth shining with spittle. "Hello, Donald, it's so very nice to meet you. My name's Charlie."

Donald gulped and Rukus frowned. "Say 'Hello, Charlie,'" Rukus said. "Remember yer manners."

"Huh, hello Charlie," Donald said.

"That's better. Now, would you like to tell me a little about yourself, Donald?"

Donald hesitated; the fear had struck him dumb.

Rukus pouted. "Oh, are you a bit shy? That's all right. How about I tell you a little about Charlie then? Would you like that?"

Donald nodded and Anthony was glad he was co-operating.

Rukus clapped his hands and leapt back onto the stage. He sat and crossed his legs, the sound of his hip joints cracking in the air.

"Okay, listen up kiddies," he said. "You won't hear a story like this every day!"

## 9

Madeline stood at the front door of her house, glaring at the main street out of Keaton and wondered when her son was going to appear.

*He's in so much trouble when he gets home:* she promised herself.

It was already dark, the points of stars beginning to emerge in the velvet sky.

*Where the hell is he?*

She checked her watch: 6:12pm.

*I bet he got kept back after school again.*

Madeline turned from the door and went to the kitchen to find the telephone. She dialed the number for the school; she knew it well, as Anthony had been kept back a number of times for not doing his homework. Deep down, she knew he did it so he didn't have to come home.

*Just wait until he gets home.*

The phone rang out. She redialed. It rang out again. No detention today.

"Damn it!"

This time she dialed the store; old man Davis answered.

"No, Maddie, haven't seen him," he said. "Is everything okay with you—"

She cut him off, immediately dialing her friend Suzie on the other side of town. Sometimes Anthony went over to Suzie's after school to play X-Box with her seven-year-old son.

"Well, he's not here," Suzie said. "Sounds like he's gonna be in a world of trouble when he turns up, though."

Six-thirty-nine and still no sign. A twinge of concern swelled in her gut and as the minutes ticked by it ballooned until she began to think horrible thoughts: of her son being kidnapped; of her husband hanging from the tree in the woods.

Madeline reached for the phone again and called the Sheriff's station. Sheriff Dawson answered on the second ring.

"It's Anthony," Madeline said. "He ain't come home."

"He ain't at a friend's, or at school?

"No, I called Suzie too and she ain't seen him either. I haven't seen him since last night when he went to bed."

Burke let out a long sigh. "Have you two been fighting again, Maddie?"

Madeline rubbed her temples. "I'm just tired, Sheriff. Tired of that boy not doing what he's told."

"Well, I ain't his momma, Maddie—that's yer job," Dawson said. "You want me to send Burke out to look for him?"

Maddie licked her lips. "Would you? Please?"

"Okay," Dawson said. "But you call me the second he walks through yer door and I'll give him a talking to."

Madeline let out a deep breath. "Thank you, Ray."

She put down the phone and went back to the front door to stare at the street, Dominic hanging in the woods still a splinter in her mind.

"This tale begins towards the end of the Civil War."

The children shivered from the cold and the dread of Rukus"s voice; his words and gestures.

"Our troupe came here in the winter of 1864," he said. "We were desperate and starving and thought the people needed some good humor; some lively entertainment. So we brought our rickety caravans here, into these woods." Rukus craned his neck upwards to consider his tomb. "Little did we know we'd never leave this accursed place."

Rukus got to his feet and danced a jig. "So there we were, dancing and singing, having a grand old time. The people were laughing and showering us with pennies. I was hilarious, warming them up for the grand finale, when all of a sudden—"

He slammed his shoe on the stage and it rang like a death knell. "Three soldiers stormed in on our show!"

Anthony leaned forwards. "Soldiers!"

Rukus stopped, genuinely surprised. "You've heard this story?"

Anthony shook his head and cringed, sickened that he was being drawn in by the monster's tale. "I just saw an old picture in the store...There were soldiers in it."

Rukus sneered. "Yes, that was probably those same fiends! They came in drunk and engorged on the horrors of the battlefield. Their grey uniforms were flecked with their countrymen's blood!" He gripped his cane so tight the children thought it would break. "And do you know what they did?"

The children dared not speak and this only raised Rukus's ire.

"They chased everyone out of the tent, that's what they did! Then we watched as they gathered up all our hard-earned money. We begged them to leave us be, but that only succeeded in spurring them on. Their sergeant—a true fiend—ordered his men to stomp on our stage, and tear our curtains, but when they tired of that, the sergeant told them to play with us."

Rukus gazed at the floorboards as if there was something beneath it.

"They wanted their own show, they said." Rukus continued. "They...wouldn't take no for an answer. They threatened us and we had little choice but to comply.

"They dragged me back onto the stage, their rifle butts in my face and back. Those awful men ordered me to perform. "Tell us a joke!" they said. "Make us laugh!"

Rukus put his hands over his face in despair and his muffled voice sounded as if he were speaking from the grave.

"I tried," he said. "Oh, how I tried."

He threw his hands down then and the children reeled from the sight of his face contorted with rage, the tears mingling with spittle.

"But I wasn't good enough, they said! So they attacked me—struck me down with their rifle butts. I tried to get up, but they just kept on hitting me and hitting me and hitting me!

"Yet that was just the beginning, children! They lifted me to my feet and while two of them held me the other...the sergeant...took his bayonet..."

Rukus took one end of the cane and pulled on it. There was a sharp snap and steel glinted in the moonlight; the steel of a short blade, much like a bayonet. Rukus tossed the scabbard end aside and gripped the handle in both hands and held it in front of his abdomen. The children shrieked as he began to stab himself all over like he was a living voodoo doll.

"And he ran me through!" Rukus cried as the first dozen wounds began to weep. "Over and over and over!"

Rukus was in a frenzy now, his stomach and chest perforated to the point of collapse. The blood trailed into the candy stripes, running down his white trousers to his shoes to mingle with the soil.

The children gaped in horror as Rukus fell to his knees. A minute passed and Rukus was slumped on the stage, his breathing drawn. Eventually the flow of blood came to a halt.

"Is he dead?" Catherine whispered, having finally opened her eyes to look.

"I don't know," Anthony said.

Suddenly Rukus's body began to shake, not with seizure, but laughter. A deep, guttural guffaw began to build inside Rukus"s wounded torso and he lifted his head to look upon his audience. Mischief blazed in his eyes and he kept laughing—at them. He jumped to his feet and slapped his knees and clapped his hands in sheer delight. Then, when he was happy with himself, he gave a low bow.

"Thank you! Thank you!" he said. "You were a wonderful audience. Alas, I must withdraw now because there is still more to the tale—too much for just one performer to tell."

He exited stage right, leaving the children once again with their dread. Cherise began to cry again, the woods lolling gently with her anguish.

"We have to try and escape," Donald said to them.

"How?" Catherine said. "These ropes are too damn tight!"

"I don't know, but we have to do something!"

"Be quiet!" Anthony said, cutting them off.

"You shut up!" Donald said, his eyes sprouting tears of anger. "I should never have come here with you. I should never have even talked to you! This is all your fault!"

"Shh!" Catherine said. "Someone's coming!"

Anthony felt a tear fall onto his own cheek as his eyes were drawn back to the stage. In the dark he saw the ghost of his father giving his son his own mournful look.

Two shadows crossed the stage. Celeste, the terrible beauty, twirled with the poise of a Russian ballerina despite the fragility of her limbs. She curtsied and then with a graceful sweep of her tethered arms, announced the entrance of her master, The Great Kaskaraken.

The magician was swathed in a cloak of fashioned darkness. Before him, he wheeled a contraption—a box, or a coffin, the children couldn't tell. It was black and lacquered to a high shine. It was simultaneously beautiful and ghastly. Kaskaraken bowed to the children, but there was only malice in his eyes. Celeste flitted around him and slipped a blotched arm into his.

"Greetings, children," Kaskaraken said. "You have heard Mr. Rukus's tale, but it is not the only event to occur on that terrible evening. The soldiers took a great interest in me and my sweet assistant, Celeste Renoir."

Celeste smiled, but quickly covered her garish mouth with the back of her hand; it seemed vanity wasn't beyond a living corpse.

"Please, you don't have to do this," Catherine cried from the audience. "If you let us go, we promise we won't tell anyone about you. We promise we'll never set foot in these woods again."

Kaskaraken waggled a finger at her. "Tut-tut-tut, young lady, you mustn't interrupt a magician when he's about to perform one of his greatest acts. Celeste, if you will, my dear."

Celeste circled him to the other side of the box. Kaskaraken opened the lid of the contraption, and his assistant climbed inside and lay down. When the magician closed the lid, all that could be seen of Celeste was her head and lower legs protruding from each end.

"The soldiers wanted me to perform magic," Kaskaraken began. "They wanted to see something remarkable—my best act. So, with nowhere to run to, I had little choice but to oblige them."

Kaskaraken retrieved a wide piece of steel from nowhere; it

was the same width and depth as the contraption. He held it over the center of the coffin-like box, all the while Celeste smiling widely at the young onlookers.

"I would never dream of revealing the mechanics of this deception to you," Kaskaraken said as he thrust the steel into the lid of the box. At first it seemed to resist him, until suddenly it emerged through the bottom with a harsh scrape of metal on wood.

"Ouch!" Celeste said, still grinning from ear to ear.

The Great Kaskaraken withdrew the steel and for a second—the blink of an eye—Anthony thought he saw blood on its edge; he hoped his eyes had deceived him. The magician took hold of both ends of the box and gently pulled it apart—into two halves. Miraculously, there was no blood, no horror to behold—only an elaborate misdirection.

"Celeste was in no danger, as you can see," Kaskaraken said.

The lovely assistant waggled her legs in one half of the box and nodded her head in the other; an invisible chain crossed the four-foot void between. The magician pushed the halves back into one and then opened the lid for Celeste to climb out—whole once more. Still smiling, she curtsied.

But even Anthony—in fact all of them—sensed something grotesque was about to occur.

"Regrettably," Kaskaraken said, "this marvel was not enough to impress the ignorant warmongers. The sergeant demanded proof. He wanted to know my secret."

Celeste began to look afraid, sheer terror in her eyes, her lips trembling. Kaskaraken reached out to her tenderly.

"Please, my darling, don't be afraid," he said, urging her to stand at his side. "The soldiers took hold of Celeste. They wanted to see her in pieces and then have me put her back together. I offered to put her in the contraption again—to repeat the trick, but lo, they expected real magic, not trickery."

He rubbed Celeste's arms, as if to warm them. "I'm so sorry, my sweet," he said. Then he turned to the children. "One of them took out his knife..."

Anthony and the children watched as a line, glaring red and

shining, began to appear on Celeste's upper arm, where the shoulder connected to the torso. It was a perfect line, the end tracking up, around and over until it met its beginning, like an ouroboros made of blood. Then another cut appeared on her upper left thigh, then her right. The invisible blade traced around her right shoulder and Celeste whimpered, feeling the agony and the horror all over again, until finally, the red line traced the circumference of her lily-white throat.

"The soldiers took her to pieces," Kaskaraken said and, as the last syllable passed his lips, Celeste's body fell apart, collapsing into a bloody heap. The children cried, Cherise's shrieks rolling up into the ancient trees. "They asked me to put her back together again, but I was a magician…not a miracle worker. So, the sergeant ordered me to disappear, too."

A perfect circle suddenly materialized between the magician's eyes and he too crumpled to the stage floor beside his constant companion. There may have been no gunshot, but wisps of smoke trailed from the wound.

From the ether, a massive velvet curtain dropped, cutting the scene and bringing a close to act one, but not the memory of what lay behind it.

Anthony begged for the show to end.

## 10

When Madeline didn't hear from Sheriff Dawson for almost an hour, she called him.

"Any sign of him?" she asked.

"I've spoken to my deputy, Maddie. They ain't seen him, but they're still looking. Where do you think he might have gone?

Madeline tried to stay calm, running her fingers through her hair, hoping subconsciously to collect the answer from between the threads.

"He could be anywhere," she told him. "When I find him, I'm gonna tan his hide."

"Well, we gotta find him first. Now think, where could he be? Is he at the skate park, or the store, or at the pool?"

Madeline shook her head. "No, no—I called the store and they ain't seen him. The boys at the skate park give him a hard time so he stopped goin', and we ain't got no money for him to go to the pool. God dammit!"

Sheriff Dawson let out a long sigh. "Okay, then. Well, if you think about it there ain't too many places he could be. Maybe he went to the waterhole or the old grain shed. I'll tell my deputy to look there. If you think of anywhere else you call me, okay?"

"Yeah, okay."

Madeline put down the receiver and instantly wanted to pick it up and beg the Sheriff to launch a full-scale search for her son. It wasn't that she didn't think the deputy was capable; she just knew the Sheriff would be more thorough.

She stared at her empty kitchen and then the doorway. Had she gone too far? Had she driven her boy away with her anger and despair? These thoughts seemed to tug at her mind and instinctively the same thoughts turned to Dominic. She glanced at the banister, to the small silver urn. Ashes and dust; her beloved reduced to ashes and dust.

Had all of her love truly died with Dominic? Did she have no more to give?

*He's your son, for god's sake, Maddie—our child! Our flesh and blood! Love him! Help him!*

She knew those thoughts were not her own; they'd been placed in her head. Maddie blinked and pressed her fingertips against her eyes. *I can almost hear him,* she thought. She stared at the urn again, her head slowly filling with more thoughts.

*Help him. He's afraid!*

Flashes of figures, scarred and bleeding on a stage amongst the trees, poured into her mind's eye; a parody of violence becoming reality, with Anthony among a group of children forced to watch it.

Madeline stumbled to a chair, her legs weak as she pictured the horrors and the urn. The montage was still there even when she squeezed her eyes shut.

*Find him! Come to me Maddie and find him!*

Madeline opened her eyes and she looked to the urn. Had Dominic just spoken to her from beyond the grave? Impossible!

Yet she felt compelled; there was a will inside her and she

knew she had to leave the house, to that place she had never set foot in since that heart-breaking day.

She pulled herself to her feet and moved quickly to the banister. She grabbed the urn in her arms like it was a child. But her real child was out there in the woods and he needed his mother. She ran out the front door, her arms tight around her lost love, silently praying to God there was still time to save the last piece of true love she had left.

Anthony could only watch as Rukus, Celeste and Kaskaraken dragged Donald, Catherine and Cherise onto the stage to become players in the monsters' sick performance.

When he looked at his father, all Anthony could see was the look of fear, as if Dominic Moore's spirit reflected what his son felt. There had to be some way to free them all from this nightmare. If he could just release himself from the ropes around his wrists and ankles, he could run for help.

The children Anthony had willingly lured to the woods were forced to their knees. The creatures had assumed their true forms now, their hideous bodies caressing the youngsters in anticipation for a feast. Donald was to be Rukus' meal; Celeste would have Catherine and Kaskaraken Cherise, which only left—

Mister Crispin walked onto the stage, his top-hat held mournfully to his chest. He could have led a funeral march into Hell with the look on his ravaged face. When he reached the center of the stage, he gazed down upon the boy who'd unwillingly helped him and smiled.

"Anthony, the boy without a daddy," he said with a hint of contempt. "Have you enjoyed our show? We've enjoyed bringing it to you. It's been quite some time since we've performed to an audience, but it's like riding a bicycle—you never forget. Never forget."

He replaced his hat and considered the other children quivering behind him.

"Still, the show isn't over yet. There's one more tale to tell and I've saved the best for last."

The other fiends chuckled and stared at Anthony. The boy knew they would leave his demise till last, to prolong his suffering, like they did his father.

"So there I was," Crispin said. "Watching my comrades dying around me; Rukus stabbed to death, Celeste cut to pieces, the Great Kaskaraken's brains splattered across the stage! I couldn't hide, though. The soldiers were determined to find me."

Anthony wanted to tell Crispin to kill him and be done with it, to end the torment, but a voice called to him from the stage—another performer hiding in the shadows.

*Listen to me, son.*

Anthony's head became heavy as each word swirled inside his mind.

*Your mother is on her way and you must be ready.*

The boy looked past Crispin—who was giving his all with his monologue—and saw his father's soul reaching out to him.

*Yes, it's me, Anthony—now listen!*

Meanwhile, Crispin raved on: "The soldiers wanted to lure me out like a rat, and that callous sergeant ordered his men to set fire to the caravan! Oh, the flames were so high!" He held his ragged face in his hands, the salty tears bleaching the skin. "They spread so fast, ate up everything like some great sea monster! I'd hidden inside a costume chest, but the wood became so hot, I had little choice but to clamber out. In the glare of the flames I found the soldiers waiting, their manic faces shining bright! They laughed at my terror and chased me up onto the stage where the flames had yet to reach. They aimed their rifles and waited."

Crispin looked at his palms; the patchwork of scars. "The sergeant said he liked our show—the private show just for them. He agreed that laughter was the best medicine." He raised his hands higher still, his gaze locked on them. "Then the sergeant passed around a liquor bottle to his men. They all took a swig, but they kept some for me. A cigarette was lit then and the burning tip was so miniscule amongst all the flames.

"The sergeant took the liquor bottle back only to hurl it at me, before he cocked his revolver and shot it. I was sprayed with glass and fragrant bourbon. I stood there trembling, dripping wet. Then the cigarette butt struck my coat."

There was an explosion of fire from Crispin's hands—a white hot flame that dripped all over his coat. It crawled down his sleeves and leapt down his trousers. Embers soared to his top-hat, driven by an invisible breath. The hat became a firework, spewing a huge column of flame several feet into the night air. The sparks rained down and an instant later Crispin's entire body was burning. Yet Crispin didn't scream—he simply bathed in the inferno.

Seared flesh and fatty smoke flooded the children's senses and lingered long after the ghostly flames dissipated. Once the smoke had cleared, Crispin emerged as if reborn.

"Now the show must sadly come to a close," Crispin said. "It's time for all of you to depart."

Rukus gripped Donald around the throat. "At last!" he said.

"No!" Catherine cried.

"You have no choice in the matter," Crispin told them as he leapt from the stage, eyes wild and fixed on Anthony. "We need to go on. We need souls. The man Moore is not enough to sustain us." He reached for Anthony, but held back when he saw the boy was unafraid. "Aren't you going to beg, plead once more for us to let you go?"

"Why don't you just leave?" Anthony said, his expression carrying a mask of defiance.

"What?" Crispin's surprise gave his hideousness a new level of distortion.

"Why are you still here, in these woods?" Anthony said.

"What do you mean, boy?"

Anthony considered the trees, as if for the first time. "You can't leave—or don't you want to?"

Crispin turned to his comrades and back again; they all wore the same look of bewilderment.

"We're trapped. Cursed!"

"So you say, but you're dead, so why don't you just cross over?"

Crispin cackled. "The soldiers slaughtered us, so shall we slaughter!"

Anthony smirked and Crispin detected something different in the boy's stance, his mannerism.

"But we didn't do anything to you. The children aren't the soldiers," Anthony told him. "They died a long time ago and at least they had the guts to accept it!"

"We need souls!" Crispin said, fist clenched and shaking. "These woods drain us!"

"Then leave them! Go hunt down the souls of the soldiers—the ones who deserve to be punished!"

"Where on earth would we look for them? As you said, they're dead!"

Anthony smiled widely. "You could try hell!"

Anthony saw Crispin recoil before his dark eyes scrutinized him. "What's gotten into you, boy? There's so much guile in you. Almost as if…"

The demon master of ceremonies turned to the stage and peered at the cage—at the revenant figure slumped between the bars. Dominic Moore's soul was asleep—or in a trance!

"How dare you!" Crispin snarled. "He's talking to his son—through him!" He turned to his troubadours, finger pointing to the cage. "Devour that wretch now!"

Rukus, Celeste and Kaskaraken let go of the children and converged on the cage. Anthony felt his father even more strongly.

*Open your heart son, just for a moment—let me in!*

Anthony thought of his father—his strong, dependable arms; his loving smile; the day at the mill—a pastiche of father and son moments that swelled inside until…

Up on the stage, Dominic's soul vanished before the demons' very eyes, the cage left empty.

"No, that's impossible!" Crispin howled. He turned to look at Anthony and saw, to his horror, the other children jumping from the stage. Anthony Moore stood tall; his father's strength shining from within.

"You can't have my son," Anthony said. "And you can't have these other children either."

"Get them!" Crispin said. His minions obeyed, rushing from the stage towards the group, but Anthony stood in front of them; their new protector.

"Anthony!" a voice resounded in the woods.

Madeline came running from the woods, silver urn in her arms. She beheld the monsters, saw the sheer terror in the other children's faces, the bravery in her son's.

"Give me the urn—now!" Anthony said.

She threw the urn in the air and it soared, rolling and turning right into her son's hands. Immediately, he removed the lid and scattered the ashes in a torrent. There was a flash of light, so bright it repelled the darkness and toppled the charging monsters to the ground.

When the light cleared, the All-American Travelling Troubadours found Dominic Moore—reanimated and whole, and dressed in a Confederate soldier's uniform—standing over them.

Dominic Moore was back from the grave, his remains and soul realigned. He seemed real enough to touch, yet he was on a plane between life and death.

Anthony gazed upon his father, saw an invisible foreign wind tousling his brown locks, glimpsed a golden glow on his chiseled face. He fit the grey woolen soldier's uniform well, even if it made no sense. He was an impossible sight, but a beautiful one. The dead man's presence left everyone—including the demons—mute, but Anthony's excitement overwhelmed him and burst from his lips.

"Dad!"

Dominic Moore turned, his smile gleaming. "Hey there, Ant. You just stay there, you hear?"

"Yes, sir!" Anthony said and grinned wildly—only his father ever called him "Ant", a nickname Dominic had bestowed upon him when he was two.

"It's good to see you again, son," Dominic said.

Madeline pushed her way through the other children to stand by Anthony. She took the boy's hand in hers. "Dominic?" she cried "Oh, my God!" She clasped her free hand over her mouth as tears of joy flowed.

"Hey, Maddie," Dominic said, his eyes filled with tenderness. "It's good you came. I was starting to run out of juice, calling to you both."

"That was…you…in my head?" Madeline said, her voice trembling. "How…how can you even be here…alive? And why are you dressed like that?"

Dominic nodded and turned to the creatures cowering at his feet. "I've got some unfinished business to attend to first, Maddie, then I'll explain." He stretched out his arm to his wife and son. "You need to stay back."

Madeline and Anthony stepped away, gathering the other children with them. The demons watched them, but it wasn't long before their eyes were back on their escaped prisoner. Mister Crispin got to his knees and grated his teeth together in anger.

"That was quite the trick you pulled, Mister Moore," Crispin said. "Almost as good as Kaskaraken. I'd love to know how you did it, before I kill you all over again!"

"You let them all go and we'll chat all you like, just you and me."

Crispin stood and smoothed down his coat. "I don't think they'll be going anywhere," he said. "I'll tell you what's going to happen. First, I'm going to tear you apart limb from limb in front of your slut wife and bastard son. Then we're all going to get the meals we were promised. When we're done, we'll be getting back on the road again—I so want to see how the world has changed."

Dominic sniggered derisively. "You're never getting out of these woods."

"What makes you think that?"

Dominic gestured to the woods. "I've got help—someone who knows you all too well; someone who's been waiting a long time for this moment."

Anthony watched Crispin study the uniform his father was wearing. While the boy couldn't see its significance, the shocking realization that surfaced behind Crispin's eyes meant the demon knew the secret all too well.

"The sergeant!" Crispin cried.

Crispin shrieked long and loud, charging headlong at Dominic, tackling him. The other demons got to their feet and scrambled after them. Anthony and Madeline cried out as Dominic rolled in the dust, fending off Crispin's nails and bites.

Anthony's heart ached as Crispin's teeth came close to his

father's face; he couldn't lose his father all over again at the hands of these monsters. The boy gasped as his father miraculously gained the upper hand, flipping Crispin over onto his back. Unfortunately, this left Dominic open to fresh attack from the other troubadours.

Rukus unsheathed his blade and stabbed it down into Dominic's shoulder. A fine blue light leaked from the wound, like air from a torn weather balloon. Dominic moaned in agony.

"Dad!"

Anthony tried to run to his father, but Madeline dragged him back. He saw fury cross his father's face, an emotion the man had rarely displayed in life. Dominic reached back and slapped Rukus across the face, shattering his jaw and careening his thin body into Celeste and Kaskaraken, sending the three of them tumbling to the ground.

Crispin reared up to sink his teeth into Dominic's throat. More soul-light spilled out, with more shrieks from the would-be hero. The children were too mesmerized to move, praying Anthony's father would somehow be victorious. Dominic seemed to sense their hope. With his gleaming essence spattering on the ground, he pinned Crispin down.

"You taste good!" Crispin howled.

"You want more? Then take it!"

Dominic closed his eyes and it was as though a hidden voice had willed him to bleed. The dazzling fluid pulsed from his throat and he imagined it becoming hot, so hot it would burst into flame at the slightest touch. It dripped onto Crispin's coat and face, igniting in an instant. The blue light crackled and sparked, transformed into ravenous tongues of fire.

"No!" Crispin cried as the fire grew. "No! No! No! Not again!"

Crispin panicked, kicking like a trapped mouse in the throes of death. The reflex only gave the flames more life and they twirled over the monster's entire body. The force pushed Dominic back and he too watched in awe as the inferno consumed Crispin in seconds. There was a powerful explosion and then the Master of Ceremonies was gone.

Dominic got to his feet, hand on his oozing throat, and glared at the other fiends.

"You're next!" he told them.

Rukus's eyes slowly narrowed on Crispin's murderer and flared with vengeance. Screaming from a dislocated maw, he ran headlong at Dominic, blade drawn. Dominic set his stance and caught Rukus's flimsy wrist, twisting it behind the demon's back and plunging it through his spine. The blade's tip birthed from his chest.

The candy stripes of his vest bled, mingling with Dominic's own ethereal blood. The light burned every black cell of Rukus's existence until he too combusted, exploding in Dominic's arms, the dust sifting through his fingers.

"No!" Kaskaraken cried, following in Rukus's stead.

Again Dominic was ready; he stretched out his right hand and the shape of a Colt revolver was made with the blue blood, cocked and ready.

"Time to make you disappear—for good this time!" he told the great magician.

The radiant weapon erupted and a sliver of light—a bullet of light—passed through the magician's skull. The surprise remained on Kaskaraken's face even after he fell to the ground, forever dead.

When he too exploded in a shower of sparks, Celeste screamed hysterically and turned to run. Dominic gave chase and cut her down with Rukus's blade. Madeline, Anthony and the children averted their eyes as he cut her apart and dripped his soul upon each piece, sending it all to hell.

And when his task was done, he turned to smile at his wife and son, only to collapse under the weight of what he'd done.

## 11

Anthony ran to his father and gripped the lapels of his blood-soaked jacket until his knuckles turned white.

"Dad? Get up!" he begged.

Dominic looked up at his son and put his hand on the boy's cheek. "You're safe now, buddy… The bad guys are all gone."

Anthony saw the pool of blue blood spreading beneath his father.

"But Dad, you're hurt!"

"Don't worry about me, Ant…I'll be okay."

Anthony pulled on Dominic's jacket. "No you won't! You're going to die and I don't want you to!"

Madeline crouched beside her son, her face slick with tears. "Anthony…"

"No, Mom—he can't die again! He can't!"

"Listen to me…"

"No!" Anthony kept trying to lift his father, but he was a dead weight.

"Ant…Ant," his father said. "Shh…Ant, it's okay…"

"Please, Dad, you have to get up!" his tears mingled with his father's blood.

"I can't, buddy. I only had enough strength…to get rid of those freaks."

"But how, Dom?" Madeline asked. "How could you have even come back?"

He closed his eyes and swallowed. Anthony watched his father's chest rising and falling; his breathing was getting slower and slower.

"The monsters…they kept my soul on ice…fed off it…but it wasn't enough," he explained. "Little did they know…I was feeding off them…at the same time."

Madeline frowned. "You've been here the whole time? Ever since…?"

Dominic nodded. "They butchered me…" He swallowed hard. "They put me…in that cage. But then he came to me…the sergeant…the sergeant who killed the troupe…all those years ago. He told…me…he'd been waiting…for me."

Madeline frowned. "What do you mean, Dom?"

"The sergeant…and his men…after they'd murdered the troupe…returned to the battlefield. Many of them…died there…but the sergeant lived on…and raised his own children…trying to redeem himself. But…he couldn't…while the troupe was trapped…here. When he finally died…his soul joined them in…the woods.

"All I could do was think of you two." He looked to Anthony. "The sergeant helped me call to you every day…hoping you'd come…and you did."

"You made me come here?" the boy said.

"I didn't…know if it would work, but the sergeant explained that…if I saw you again it would…give me the strength to escape. I'm sorry I put you through all this…but it was all I could think to do."

"Who is this sergeant?" Madeline asked, desperate for answers.

"His name…was Moore…Sebastian Moore," Dominic said, half-smiling and looking to his son. "You're great…great…grandfather."

Dominic let out a series of ragged coughs and Anthony saw to his horror that his father's suit jacket now looked two sizes too big.

"Can't we do anything?" Anthony cried.

Dominic shook his head. "I'm so sorry buddy…not my call. You have to understand…I was never coming back for good."

Anthony wiped his eyes, but his vision continued to blur as tears replaced tears.

"What am I going to do now, Dad?"

"You've got your mom and she's got you. You two…have to look after each other."

Madeline reached out and stroked her husband's hair; there was ash on her fingertips when she pulled it away.

"Thank you. Thank you for coming back to save our boy."

Dominic smiled. "He can save you too, Maddie…if you let him."

Madeline sobbed a wave of pent-up grief. "Oh Dom," she said. "Tell me what you were doing out here in the woods. Why were you here?"

For a moment, Dominic's face was a mask of shame, but he took in one last breath of courage.

"The mill," he said, with barely a whisper. "I got…I was…laid off. I couldn't find a way…to tell you…so I came here to think."

"Dominic, you know it wouldn't have mattered—as long as we were all together," Madeline told him. "We would always find a way."

Dominic nodded in understanding, but his head began to loll on his shoulders; consciousness fading. His lips curled at one corner though, the barest of smiles.

"Take care…" he told them.

Breath left him then and Anthony watched his father's chest collapse. Stricken, Anthony threw his arms around Dominic in the tightest of embraces. Madeline bent to kiss her husband's cheek.

"I love you," she said.

Before their eyes, Dominic Moore crumbled and broke—dust to dust, ashes to ashes.

Finally free.

A week went by before Anthony's mother said he could go back to school. Monday morning was one of sunshine, which bathed every nook and cranny of the Moore home.

Anthony bounded down the stairs into the kitchen, where he found his mother preparing lunch. She wore a pretty floral full-length dress, her luscious dark hair tied back in a ponytail. She greeted him with the brightest of smiles.

"Hey there," she said. "I hope you like peanut butter and jelly—it's all we've got at the moment until I go to town."

Anthony matched her smile. "Yeah, that's great. Thanks, Momma."

He grabbed the lunchbox and put it in his schoolbag. He was thinking about the day—the possibility of making new friends—when he felt his mother's fingers in his hair. He leant into her touch and wrapped his arms around her waist. It was their first embrace in more than a year.

"I love you, Mom," he told her.

He looked up and watched a solitary tear roll down her cheek. "I love you too, Anthony."

With that, Anthony walked out the door and ran up the street towards Keaton town. He gave her one last smile over his shoulder and turned the corner. He waited, craning his neck, and gazed back around the corner to the front door of his house, full of anticipation. A minute passed before his mother emerged and bounded down the stairs, the silver urn cradled in her arms.

Anthony saw that smile on her face then; the smile born from love. Then he heard her say:

"Come on, Dom. Let's take a walk in the woods."

Anthony knew then that although his father was gone, his spirit would always be with them; that everything would be okay.

# ABOUT THE AUTHOR

Bram Stoker Award® and multiple Australian Shadows Award nominee Greg Chapman is a horror author and artist based in Queensland, Australia.

Greg is the author of several novels, novellas and short stories, including his award-nominated debut novel, *Hollow House* and collections, *Vaudeville and Other Nightmares* and *This Sublime Darkness and Other Dark Stories*.

He is also a horror artist and designer and his first graphic novel *Witch Hunts: A Graphic History of the Burning Times* (McFarland & Company) written by authors Rocky Wood and Lisa Morton, won the Superior Achievement in a Graphic Novel category at the Bram Stoker Awards® in 2013.

He was also the President of the Australasian Horror Writers Association from 2017-2020.

## Greg Chapman's Published Work:

NOVELS
Hollow House
The Noctuary: Pandemonium
Netherkind

NOVELLAS
Torment
The Noctuary
Vaudeville
The Last Night of October
The Followers

COLLECTIONS
Vaudeville and Other Nightmares
This Sublime Darkness and Other Dark Stories
Bleak Precision
Midnight Masquerade